TABLE FOR 3

A CHARITY ANTHOLOGY

DOUGLAS FORD   HOLLY RAE GARCIA
REBECCA ROWLAND

Edited by
HOLLY RAE GARCIA

EASTON FALLS

Copyright © 2023 by Easton Falls Publishing

All rights reserved.

ISBN: 978-1-7369432-7-4

Cover Design: Holly Rae Garcia

No part of this book may be produced in any form or by any electronic, mechanical, or artificial intelligence system means, including information storage and retrieval systems, without permission in writing from the publisher, except by a reviewer who may use brief quotations in a book review.

The characters and events in this book are fictitious.
Any similarity to real persons, living or dead, is
coincidental and not intended by the author.

Authors retain copyright of individual stories.

EASTON FALLS
PUBLISHING

PRAISE FOR TABLE FOR 3

Being constantly hungry can make a person desperate. These three authors explore what horrors could transpire in a society where *everyone* is hungry *all the time* - an all too real possibility given the climate crisis the world is grappling with.

— BEV VINCENT, AUTHOR OF *STEPHEN KING: A COMPLETE EXPLORATION OF HIS WORK, LIFE, AND INFLUENCES*

More than food for thought, Table for 3 is powerful, provocative, and deeply disturbing.

— CANDACE NOLA, AWARD-WINNING AUTHOR & EDITOR

This trio of tales is sinister and disturbing, a perfectly seasoned course of hunger-themed horror that packs an emotional punch!

— JEREMY HEPLER, AUTHOR OF *THE BOULEVARD MONSTER*

CONTENTS

Foreword   vii

THE LAST SLAUGHTER   1
Douglas Ford

CAT FOOD   87
Holly Rae Garcia

ROCK OF AGES   171
Rebecca Rowland

Texas Food Bank Information   251

FOREWORD

Millions of families in the United States face food insecurity related to poverty and the proliferation of food deserts where access to food is severely limited. One would think hunger would be eradicated in this grand state of Texas—the largest farming state in the country—where green space exists almost everywhere one looks and farming is a predominant way of life.

This is not the case. According to the organization Feeding America, one in seven people face hunger and one in six children are hungry.

Of the three basic needs historically outlined as necessary for human well-being (in recent times, this list has been expanded to include other elements required to measure poverty), food is by far the most critical. Without food, a person simply cannot function. Fatigue can set in, bringing brain fog and irritability along with it. A starving person can then begin to obsess over food thoughts and become perpetually lightheaded. Other debilitating physical symptoms of starvation manifest in the last stages: rapid heart rate, muscle wasting, and an immune system rendered ineffective.

Foreword

There are few things as torturous as unrelenting hunger pangs and the escalation of starvation throbbing and eating away deep within a body that requires sustenance for every basic function. The symptoms of starvation are painful. Hunger is frightening. The extended longing for sustenance is horrific.

And right at the edge of the atrocities undergirding humankind's acceptance of food shortages in some communities exist the narratives in this book, somehow nearly as mortifying as the existence of starvation. The harrowing stories comprising this anthology hold up as both freestanding nightmares, oozing fetid darkness, then intertwining to create a new magnification of the pain and effects of prolonged hunger, resulting in perpetuating the overpowering need to sob hoarsely in despair. Each details our society's route along the road towards an existence of selfish hoarding where starvation will be bestowed many people, despite the abundance of resources.

It is necessary that we engage with Douglas Ford's The Last Slaughter and immerse ourselves in a world where unholy alliances must be made in order to guarantee provisions for those who believe. Cat Food by Holly Rae Garcia extends this realm by offering a glimpse at the things people faced with extreme food shortages, without such alliances, might be willing to risk in order to meet that need. Rebecca Rowland's Rock of Ages rounds out the experience with terrifying psychological effects of ongoing hunger that could very well usher in a new world order we should not want to see: one propelled by scarcity, need, and madness.

These tales will make the reader want to look away from these stories—from the gore, sorrow, pain, and fear—to deny that hunger prevails unnecessarily. Resist this urge and face the issue. Humankind should not become complacent in the face of increasing numbers of fellow beings suffering from starvation. The breakdown of the sufferers will quickly spell the devolution of all.

RJ Joseph
April 2023

THE LAST SLAUGHTER

by Douglas Ford

This one is dedicated to Jerlin

1

John Teecar knew the truth, even if no one besides his mother, Laura, ever said it out loud: Pinky Randall was his father.

That Pinky Randall, the richest man in town. So rich that Laura Teecar's parents didn't require a chaperone when he came calling upon her soon after she turned sixteen. Her birthday came in August, and the Swine Awards took place every Autumn. At least until food became scarce and the land went dry.

But in those days, before people started going hungry, people owed their livelihoods to land-owners like the Randalls. Good stock came from that family, just like the beef they harvested in their slaughterhouses and the bacon cut from their fattened hogs. Who could blame Mr. and Mrs. Teecar if they thought that Pinky Randall had only the most honorable intentions with their daughter?

John knew the story by heart—how Pinky Randall showed up in a shiny pink convertible and wearing polished wing-tip shoes, all untarnished by the blood floors of his family's killing rooms. He beamed at Mr. and Mrs. Teecar from where

The Last Slaughter

he sat on their living room sofa, his hands folded neatly in his lap. How they fussed over him, for having a member of the Randall family in one's living room practically amounted to playing host to royalty. John's grandmother, Mrs. Teecar, kept asking him over and over if he'd like a glass of sweet tea.

"No ma'am," Pinky Randall said each time, acting as if he'd heard the question for only the first time. "I'm saving room for the banquet. You do have such a nice home, Mr. Teecar."

John's grandfather smiled back from his usual place in his recliner. He sat on it every evening after coming home from a busy day of caring for livestock, often so tired that he fell asleep within moments of leaning back. He put in hard hours, but it kept food on the table in those days before everything went into decline. That didn't stop his expression from looking haunted at times. Understandable when you consider how his job involved spilling blood from living things, even calves newly separated from their mother for their fine meat. He would die just one year later, the result of a heart attack, but fortunately he lived long enough to see the birth of his bastard grandson. A good employee, he never breathed a word about what Pinky Randall did.

"I'm honored to hear those words," Mr. Teecar said. He didn't lean back in his recliner with such a refined visitor in his home. To do so would suggest disrespect, even if his age at 54 almost doubled that of his esteemed guest. A member of the Randall family might smile as if they did not perceive an insult, but rest assured they noticed every gesture and would find a way to redress any slight aimed in their direction. Mr. Teecar didn't want to find himself shoveling shit vacated from the bowels of dying animals. He knew that lowering the backrest of his chair and raising his feet could have that unintended consequence.

The Last Slaughter

Smiling politely, Pinky Randall declined two more offers of a glass of sweet tea. Each new offer made by Mrs. Teecar made her husband flinch, for one could never reliably anticipate what might insult a member of the Randall dynasty, especially its heir.

In truth, Mr. and Mrs. Teecar could not wait for their daughter to emerge from her bedroom so that her date with this important man could finally commence and they could breathe easily again. When she eventually did appear, she stood before them wearing her pink communion dress, a choice made in honor of Pinky's name at the suggestion of her mother.

Evidently, that decision met his approval because Pinky smiled and licked his lips. "Why, you look fine, Laura. Almost as beautiful as your dear mother."

Mrs. Teecar blushed at this remark. Meanwhile, her husband broke out in sweat, his nervousness now painfully manifest.

"She's wearing that in honor of you," said Laura's mother. Then she repeated her statement as if no one heard her the first time, and the sweat on Mr. Teecar's forehead became all the more palpable.

"Well, now," said Pinky Randall, "I must make my own tribute in return. What shall that be?" He demonstrated his careful deliberation by wrinkling his brow and tapping his chin. Then he snapped his fingers. "I know! The hog I intend to enter into this year's swine competition. You know the animal I refer to, don't you, Ralph?"

Despite Mr. Teecar's seniority, Pinky Randall always referred to him by his first name. Ralph Teecar shifted in his seat, uncomfortable with the turn in direction just taken by the conversation. Of course he knew the hog, a prized specimen kept in a special pen. "I do," he finally said.

9

The Last Slaughter

Pinky Randall's expression showed no evidence that he found his host's hesitation too long or impolite. Still grinning, his eyes marched up and down Laura's fine form. He said, "I'll name that hog after your sweet daughter."

Quiet hung over the room. Perhaps no one knew what to say. Finally, Mrs. Teecar clapped her hands. "Well, isn't that an honor. It is, isn't it, Laura? You heard what Mr. Randall just said."

But Laura didn't speak. She regarded first her parents and then Pinky Randall with a blank expression. The sweat trickled down Mr. Teecar's forehead and burned his eyes. He fumbled in his pockets for a handkerchief, but he couldn't find one.

"What do you say to that, you fine thing?" asked Pinky Randall.

"What do you say to that, girl?" her father asked.

Though she mumbled, her words indistinct, no one missed the inflection at the end of her reply. But if that bothered Pinky Randall, he carried such good breeding that he didn't allow it to show. "Well now," he said, "we've got to be on our way." He offered his arm to Laura, and an awkward moment ensued when she hesitated, evidently not sure how to accept such a formal gesture, especially from a suitor with the grace and sophistication of Pinky Randall.

Laura's mother saw them to the door, and even Ralph Teecar rose from his recliner to shake the younger man's hand one last time. His palms felt moist, an obvious fact to everyone when Pinky Randall wiped his hand on his pants leg.

"Rest assured, I'll have her home at a respectable hour," said Pinky Randall just before opening the passenger door of his convertible and assisting Laura inside. Mr. and Mrs. Teecar waved as the car departed in a cloud of dust. Only then did they look at one another. Ralph Teecar saw the tears in his wife's eyes.

"Stupid fucking woman," he said.

He spoke these words in a growl so low that Mrs. Teecar thought she misheard him. When she turned to him, she saw a look of pure loathing in his expression.

"You just babbled like an idiot," he said. "Did you not understand the first time that the man *did not want your goddamn tea*?"

She hardly knew what to say. "I only asked him once," she said finally, though she knew she asked him many times. "Did I offend him?"

"*Did I offend him?* You most certainly did offend him." Feeling a slight pang in his chest—the first sign of the blockage that would kill him in just over a year—Ralph Teecar returned to his living room and slumped into his recliner.

"You did nothing to help the situation," Mrs. Teecar said. "All you did was sit there." She bit her lip. "If we truly offended Mr. Randall—"

"You mean, if *you* offended him," her husband said.

"—then he'll still bring Laura home on time, won't he? He won't... I mean, he'll bring her home, won't he?" She couldn't identify the ominous fear that came over her. She silently reminded herself of the pedigree of the Randall family. Pinky Randall had money, and people with money never did dishonorable things. Having money meant a blessing from the Lord, and He didn't bestow fortune on the unworthy or profane.

"Damn stupid woman," said Ralph Teecar. Then he used the television remote to turn on that evening's game show. Then they watched a series of sitcoms that failed to make either of them laugh, and finally, the evening news came on. Before long, they struggled to remain awake while Johnny

The Last Slaughter

Carson made jokes at the expense of the president. Not one word between them the entire time, even well after the respectable hour came and went without Pinky Randall's convertible appearing in their driveway.

Nor did they speak right away when Laura herself stumbled through the door, her face wet with tears and sweat. The torn strap of her pink dress hung from her bare shoulder, and the light of the television revealed her bleeding lips and blackened left eye. Later, while helping Laura undress and step into the shower, Mrs. Teecar saw the teeth marks on her daughter's breasts and the torn flesh between her thighs.

As he waited in the hallway, the sweats hit Ralph Teecar something awful. That fluttering in his chest felt out of control, and he dreaded the next time he would see Pinky Randall at work. For all he knew, he would find himself unemployed in the morning. "Stupid woman," he said once more, even though his wife stood outside the range of hearing as she helped her daughter clean off the blood and the dirt. "Goddamn stupid."

2

Before he reached full adulthood, John Teecar knew these details by heart, and though he never had the opportunity to know him personally, he felt as if he had developed an intimate knowledge of his grandfather's personality. He held his memory in high regard, considering him a saint amongst men and too good to live long in this world. His grandfather spent his short life earning an honest living at Randall Meats, but all he had to show for it was a crumbling gravestone with his last name incorrectly spelled with two r's instead of one:

Rudolph C. Teecarr
Loving Father and Husband
Faithful Employee of Randall Meats

"See that?" his mother would say on the occasions when they drove together to the cemetery to lay flowers upon his grandfather's final resting place. "That's the only thing that ties your daddy's name to yours." She drew upon her cigarette and released a long plume of smoke, a habit she developed a month after she gave birth to John Teecar, once she knew that the world would never show her any kindness. "Never doubt the truth, no matter how much they try to deny it. You are a Randall."

John picked up a sizeable chunk of gravestone that had broken away. Cheap granite, apparently, not even marble. Other fragments lay strewn on the grass, broken off as a result of some truancy, maybe a Halloween prank. He gripped the broken piece as he listened to his mother's pronouncement, one she repeated for as long as he could remember. Perhaps as early as a toddler, stumbling his way through the gravestones. As a gangly teenager, he began to grasp the significance of what his mother told him regarding his true parentage, especially as he bore witness to how the rest of the town bowed down before the privileged feet of the Randall legacy. That awareness evolved into resentment as he closed in on his twenties. Though only sixteen years his senior, his mother looked much older, thanks to the effects of poverty and the Pall Malls.

"I used to be pretty," she liked to tell him as he grew older. "You know that, right?"

"You're still pretty," he always said in reply.

"Bullshit," she'd say, but she would reach over and squeeze his shoulder.

After visiting the cemetery, they'd drive past the main processing building for Randall Meats. In recent years, it had grown quiet as the effects of a long drought persisted, the worst in several generations. For miles in every direction, one saw fields covered in dead grass and dried waterbeds.

Dust coated the air, which they now attributed to Laura's worsening cough. They rolled up the windows and suffered through the inside heat of the vehicle. Because of the coughing, John did most of the driving. "Go ahead and roll down your window," she said. "I'm going to cough either way. Damn allergies."

The Last Slaughter

Both of them knew the coughing had nothing to do with allergies.

"Let's go up a ways further. I want to see if anyone's tending your granddaddy's old post." Laura pointed toward an old service road, and John complied, though he thought he ought to get them home so she could rest. The longer they stayed out, the worse the coughing became.

The road took them to what looked like a series of outbuildings, where Ralph Teecar once oversaw the more prized livestock, including more than one winner of the Swine Awards. "There," Laura said once it came into view. "That's where it happened. Where you were conceived. Where Pinky Randall kept his prized pigs." She tried laughing, but that only resulted in more coughing. When it subsided, she said in a croaking voice, "Laura. He still named it after me, you know. The swine."

John nodded, though he didn't know if she referred to the animal or to Pinky Randall. He stared at the building, willing himself not to cry. He wanted to use his mother's lighter to set that building aflame, perform a mad dance as he watched it burn. His hands gripped the wheel, wondering if he could ever summon the courage to perform this act.

"Alright." Once more his mother squeezed his shoulder. "Time to go. Remember to keep the windows down." She lit another Pall Mall, and the car filled with smoke as they lumbered back up the service road. No air moved through the open windows. When they reached the intersection, John pressed the brake and let the car idle. Then he faced his mother.

"One more stop," he said.

She raised an eyebrow in reply, but she sensed what he had in mind. John turned right instead of left. He followed the curve of the county road until it brought them to a wooden fence. Beyond that, a line of oaks. On the former site of an antebellum plantation now sat a garish, three-story mansion. The gate that guarded his driveway hung open. John drove slowly so as not to arouse suspicion, aware that the old compact car made labored noises, its pistons and gears doomed to fail at any moment. *Just a little further. Don't die here*, he thought. His mother smoked as the Randall manor home came into view.

"Do what you're going to do fast," she said. "I don't want to be caught dead here." She flicked her cigarette out the window as John stopped the car. She watched him as he gripped the piece of broken granite from his grandfather's gravestone and exited the vehicle. She looked for cameras as John walked to within minimum distance of a plate glass window overlooking the driveway, where he reared back and threw the granite with all his might. Then came the sound of shattered glass and from somewhere distant, an alarm.

As John walked briskly back to the car, she lit another cigarette. They watched the dashboard with anticipation, wondering if the car would even start again. Laura exhaled smoke through her nostrils. "Next time, keep it running." John ignored the remark, trying a second time and then a third time. On the fourth try, the engine finally started, and they peeled away with a screech of the tires, the alarm still ringing behind them.

3

Surprisingly, committing this lawless act did nothing to change how John felt about his circumstances. When they returned home, he saw the same squalor waiting them, a decades-old house fallen into disrepair due to lack of money and resources, as well as the same lifeless pasture and the same empty pantry, save what they could cobble together from food stamps and hand-outs at the local food bank. Even worse, they returned to the same mute occupant who shared the house with them: John's grandmother, limited to a sad existence in bed after the stroke she suffered on John's sixteenth birthday.

Though the stroke robbed her of speech and mobility, her heart continued to beat soundly and reliably, steadfast in its refusal to give up. John visited her daily, assisting her with her bodily needs and talking to her, sometimes answering for her when he asked her questions.

He sat near now while outside the window, his mother spoke to the deputy who showed up to inquire about the broken window at the Randall residence. Silently, he held his grandmother's hand in his lap, wondering if the deputy would

The Last Slaughter

take him to jail. His grandmother's hand squeezed his, though whether from reflex or sympathy, John couldn't tell.

Eventually, the deputy drove away, and his mother joined him in the bedroom.

"We need to move her before she gets a new bedsore," Laura said. "Help me out."

John complied. As usual, he observed how his mother treated his grandmother with rough hands, grabbing and pinching without regard for the woman's comfort. He tried to balance that with extra gentleness. Without conversation, they adjusted the old woman's position, John waiting for her to report on what the deputy said. The possibility of jail made him anxious. Finally, her silence forced him to ask.

She snapped her reply at him. "No. You're not going to jail. Just get over yourself."

Though not a stranger to unexpected spikes in his mother's temper, they still hurt nonetheless, even when she softened quickly, as she did now.

"He wouldn't take you to prison," she said. "He's sweet on me. He just wanted to know if I wanted to go out to dinner with him this Saturday. I told him I had other gentleman callers." She smiled. "Don't you see them lining up outside?"

John forced himself to smile. "What did you really say?"

"He asked me if I was Laura Teecar. I said, 'Yeah, that's me. Pinky Randall's prized pig.' He said he was here to investigate an act of vandalism, and I said I didn't know anything about it. I told him to tell Pinky Randall to come face us like a man. I said that if he weren't a no-good coward that he could finally meet his son in person. Remind him, I said, that we live down the road and that he can come say hello himself rather than send some limp-dick deputy instead."

"Am I or am I not going to jail?"

"No, you're not going to jail. Pinky Randall doesn't have the balls to press charges. He'd have to face us. Face you."

Later, John found himself dozing on the recliner in front of the television. Each night he slept on the recliner that once belonged to Ralph Teecar, his usual spot since his grandmother had one room while his mother had the other. When it chose to work, the television provided him with a kind of lullaby every night, helping him shut out the rest of the world. Just before he could slip away into sleep, he heard a knock at the door.

Dressed only in his underwear, he answered and found the deputy on the other side of the door.

"You dress that way around your mother?" the deputy asked.

John pinched the fly of his boxers to keep them closed. "Hold on, I'll get my pants." He assumed the deputy came to take him to jail, but before he could get one leg into his trousers, his mother came into the room wearing a negligee he'd never in his life seen.

"You're late," she said to the deputy, who now stood inside the doorway.

"Rufus Birdwell fell into his septic tank," said the deputy.

Laura looked at the deputy, and John looked at how much thigh her negligee revealed. "Do I know Rufus Birdwell?"

"Doesn't matter," the deputy said. "He's dead now. Methane killed him." The deputy looked at John. "Only takes three or four minutes of breathing it before it kills your brain. We had to fish him out. I needed a shower."

"Very considerate of you." Laura motioned to her son. "Turn up that TV." Then she led the way to her room, the deputy glancing back at John with a shit-eating grin.

John didn't turn up the volume of the television. Instead, he endured every gasp, every moan, every sigh that came from his mother's room, and he didn't sleep a wink all night. A just punishment, he decided, considering that he could only blame himself for throwing that cheap piece of granite.

He just wished it hit someone when he threw it and split their skull open.

4

After some time, he decided he couldn't take any more and that he needed to leave. He had a destination in mind, too. If he had to serve some form of penance, he would do something that truly warranted it. Upon getting dressed, he took the car keys, and after considering it for a few moments, he also took his mother's cigarette lighter. Before driving off, he went into their run-down shed and found some cloth rags, along with an old metal gas container he used to fill the lawn mower on the occasions that it worked.

Then he left quickly just to make sure he wouldn't have to see the deputy's shit-eating grin again. If he saw the man's face again, he might pound it into a pulpy mess. Then it wouldn't matter who his mother decided to fuck. Nothing he could do about it from a jail cell.

Or Death Row. Jail scared him, but nothing froze his blood like the thought of Death Row.

As he drove toward his destination, he thought of what his mother said to him once. *We do for family what we sometimes wouldn't do for just ourselves.* Maybe that explained the disgusting act she decided to perform with the deputy. Not for

The Last Slaughter

herself—how could she possibly desire the deputy of all people?—but for him.

Somehow that only seemed to enrage him more. It made him feel guilty. And dirty.

To get rid of those feelings, he needed to do something for her.

As he used his last ten dollars to fill the gas can, he watched the moon climb up over the horizon and into a cloudless sky. Then he drove toward Randall Meats, his father's empire as well as his birthright, though he would never inherit it. His route took him once more past his grandfather's final resting place.

Along the way, he considered burning down Pinky Randall's house, but he decided against it, balking at the idea of killing the people inside it. He didn't know for certain, but he suspected that Pinky kept a staff, probably a butler and gaggle of maids that answered to his every whim and need. Killing them would surely hand him on Death Row, and he wouldn't have a single argument to make in his own defense. *Yeah, I did it*, he'd say to the judge before the gavel fell. And they'd catch him for sure. After the window incident, Pinky probably installed cameras everywhere.

Instead, he considered burning down Randall Meats itself, that concrete monstrosity overlooking a dead land. He suspected that it stood empty now, many of its employees let go in the name of downsizing. With feed becoming scarcer and more expensive, so did meat products, and everyone except the very wealthy slowly starved in a dwindling environment. The apocalypse could not happen fast enough for John. If the planet was burning like they said (and John had no reason to doubt it), then it sure was taking its damn time. Better to just have a rock fall from space and kill everyone all at once.

The Last Slaughter

In the end, he decided to leave Randall Meats standing. He suspected his ten dollars couldn't buy enough gasoline to bring down the whole thing, and he truly did want a fiery spectacle and as much devastation as he could buy with American money.

Then he got a better idea: that outbuilding where his grandfather once worked. Where *it* happened. Where Pinky Randall violated his mother and planted the seed that would one day become John.

He made the turn and soon enough came in sight of his target. It sat dark and quiet, probably like the day Pinky took his mother to see his prized pig, the one he named in her "honor."

John heard the story enough times that he knew it by heart —how Pinky talked on and on about that pig as he drove his mother to the banquet dinner, where all the other big-wigs in the food industry gathered for a giant feast so they could compare their respective bank accounts. Laura still found herself disbelieving that Pinky would choose her as his date, and she could barely contain herself as she thought about the smorgasbord awaiting her. At the time, Laura loved food, but hated enduring her mother's criticisms of her appetites. *Don't eat so much or you'll get fat. Then no man will marry you*, Laura's mother used to say. And Laura believed it, just as she once believed she would one day find happiness through marriage. Maybe she allowed herself to imagine nuptials with Pinky Randall himself.

Pinky promised Laura they would make it a short stop. She had no interest in meeting a pig, especially one not already prepared for feasting. Having one named after her certainly didn't make it special. No way did it make *her* feel special. If anything, she ought to feel insulted, but this date and what it symbolized meant so much to her parents, and she didn't want

The Last Slaughter

to disappoint them. She especially wanted to avoid her father's disappointment, though she never specified the reason for that.

In those days, Laura struggled to express herself, a problem she no longer experienced. John could count as truth whatever words passed through her lips, or so he reflected as he stopped the car a safe distance away and began gathering the rags along with the gas can. He imagined how the scene would have looked all those years ago, Pinky stopping his convertible on this very spot and taking Laura by the hand. *Only a few minutes, you'll see,* he likely promised as he led her to the entrance of the outbuilding. According to Laura, she'd come to this building before a few times prior to this occasion, always in the company of her mother to bring her father something he'd forgotten, often his lunch, but he never allowed her to see what they kept on the inside. Her father always met them at the car, and if Laura expressed any desire to see the interior of the building, he would shake his head impatiently. *You can't,* he'd say, *Mr. Randall won't allow it. You can't even tell anyone you've been here.* Then he'd look at his wife meaningfully. *I might get fired.*

John imagined how these words would have wounded Laura's daughterly devotion. She craved her father's attention. When she found him fast asleep on his recliner, she would sometimes crawl in next to him, snuggling close to him all the way until the morning sun rose. How it must have offended her to see her father keep something so private, not even opening the door for her to take even a peek, but standing there waving at them until they finally drove away.

Undoubtedly, Laura kept these occasions to herself as Pinky Randall unlocked this very door so that she could gaze upon his special pig. How special? Pinky couldn't wait for her to see. He winked at her as he invited her to step inside.

The Last Slaughter

Was there even a pig? John pondered this question as he trudged up a short incline, arms weighed down by his supplies. His mother's answer to this question always involved inconsistencies. Sometimes she claimed to have seen the swine just before Pinky wrestled her to the ground, and she found the animal unimpressive. Other times she confessed that she could see very little, though she sensed other eyes watching as she finally managed to fight her way out from underneath Pinky's weight, eventually stumbling outside with him calling after her. She stayed away from the road as she made the perilous trek home, avoiding headlights and the sound of tires, believing that Pinky would come after her with the intention of doing her serious harm.

Recollecting this story, John determined that he'd chosen his target correctly. A quiet stillness hung over the scene and burning down this horrid place would bring a certain symbolic satisfaction both to him and to his mother. He would also avoid, he believed, serious legal jeopardy. If the deputy came to arrest him, John would pose a simple question: why on earth would he burn down such a useless building? Of course, his mother had her own way of handling the deputy, but he wanted to avoid that. He hated thinking of his hands all over her.

Wooden boards covered the few windows on the main side of the building. Each piece of plywood bore strange markings, a strange sort of graffiti by the look of it, certainly not in a language he recognized—just loops, lines, and dots, denoting a symbolism foreign to his intelligence. Perhaps gang markings, though he knew of no gangs in their community. When he stepped closer to examine it more closely, the sound of crunching came from beneath his feet. He stepped back, thinking he'd stepped in glass, but it looked like something else. Sand perhaps, or more likely rock salt. Someone tossed

The Last Slaughter

heaps of salt along the outside the building, even in front of the door. That door, he assumed, would be locked, but he had no interest in testing that assumption.

Instead, he began soaking the rags in gasoline. Then he stuffed them between the boards and the cheap siding of the building. He'd never burned down a building, so he acted on instinct rather than knowledge or experience. The rags, he figured, would act as wicks, and once he had them spaced well enough, he would light them while giving his legs enough time to carry him far enough away to avoid any potential injury—but not too far that he couldn't enjoy the spectacle.

As he finished soaking the last rag, he thought he heard a voice calling out from the distance. Impulsively, he ducked. Crouching, he waited in anticipation, hopeful that it was just his nerves playing tricks on his senses.

When he heard nothing more, he quickly emptied the rest of the gasoline onto the salt heaped around the doorway, no longer putting any thought or deliberation into his actions. He needn't have bothered with the rags, he decided. He spent so much time wedging them in place. On the other hand, he needed something to ignite with the lighter, so they served their purpose. He took out his mother's lighter and started to flick its wheel.

But he heard the voice again. No more doubting the accuracy of his senses.

A woman's voice, calling for help.

He stood frozen, the lighter gripped in his right hand, trying to determine its source. He waited as the seconds ticked by, knowing somehow that he would hear it again. And he did.

"Help me."

Now he knew its point of origin—from behind one of the boarded windows, someone pleading for help.

No telling what Pinky Randall used the building for nowadays. As far as John could tell, it stood in disrepair, dilapidated, even if it once housed the pigs Pinky used to win his collection of Swine Awards, including one such animal named Laura. He had no reason to believe that the owner of that voice posed a threat to him. On the contrary, they needed his help.

"Where are you?" he called out. "Keep talking." He moved past the stinking rags, waiting for a reply.

"Trapped in here," said the voice. "Let me out."

Now John could tell—it came from the plywood covering the last window. Once more, something crunched under his feet as he pressed his ear against the barrier. From the other side, he imagined he could hear sounds of desperate breathing.

"I'm going to get you out," he said, and he began pacing back and forth, not at all sure how he would manage that feat. Then he remembered—the car, parked a short distance away, contained what he needed: a spare tire accompanied by a heavy bar of iron. "Wait here," he said to whoever called out to him from inside the building.

Not that the person could go *anywhere* without his help. Probably someone kept prisoner by Pinky Randall, he reckoned. Maybe someone he kept chained to the wall, forced to endure perverted acts.

As he stumbled toward the car, he forgot all about the lighter and the gasoline. At least until lightning filled the sky. He reminded himself that it almost never rained anymore, the land around them so dry and brittle that hardly anything grew there, hastening the decline of Randall Meats.

Which would be just fine with him, if not for the fact that it meant everyone else in the community would slide deeper into poverty. That never seemed to change Pinky's circumstances though, living in that fine house up the street.

The Last Slaughter

Once more lightning filled the sky, and John felt a twinge of fear as he reached the car. What if a bolt of lightning struck the building, igniting the gasoline and causing it to go up in flames with the woman stuck inside it? He found the tire iron and hastened his return, flinching with each lightning flash.

"I'm back!" he called out as he began working to pry loose the board, the sand or the salt or whatever grating beneath his shoes. As he labored, he noticed something else about the strange designs scrawled on the wood. Whoever put them there used, not paint but charcoal. He never heard of a gang that used such material. One good rainstorm and it would all come off.

Then again, what rain? he thought.

At first, he didn't think he'd ever pry the board loose. Someone used bolts rather than simple nails.

"Get me out of here," he heard the voice say.

It sounded more like a girl than a woman. He renewed his efforts with greater determination. Why didn't someone like him come to his mother's rescue all those years ago when Pinky defiled her? Where were the good people when you needed them?

Right here, he said to himself. *You're one of the good people.* Then he made one more pull, and finally, the board came free with a groan.

He pushed it aside so he could assess the next obstacle.

And he saw none. Just an opening that might have once held a stall door of some sort.

Darkness spilled from the opening. Even a flash of heat lightning did nothing to dispel it.

All thoughts of leaping in heroically fell to the wayside. Instead, he hesitated.

He spoke to the darkness. "You in there?"

"Yes," came the response. A quiet voice, almost as if she

now feared him. And maybe she had good reason for mistrusting a stranger. He shuddered to imagine what she experienced in there.

"I'm going to save you," he said.

But the darkness coiled around him, and he failed to move.

"Okay," said the voice.

That spurred him into motion. He stepped over the line of salt and into the building.

Under his feet, the floor felt pliant. Hay, he surmised. Unable to see, he fumbled again for the lighter, but the flame did little to dispel the darkness.

What he could see looked unkept and in disrepair, the hay filthy. The noxious odor of human waste rose around him, and he unsuccessfully tried to stifle it by covering his nose.

The buzzing of flies led him to a corner where he found the girl.

Her appearance in the lighter's flame startled him. Not simply because of her nakedness, but also the insects that hovered about her, attracted by her filth, as well as the odor that he now knew originated with her. She huddled there with her knees drawn up to her chest, and her huge black eyes glittered in the light cast by his flame. Tangled hair lay matted against her skull, but he still felt his loins stirring in her presence. He wondered what sort of monster could keep a human being imprisoned in such squalor. Of course, he knew the answer: a monster like Pinky Randall. He thanked his mother's lucky stars that at least she'd escaped.

"Hungry," the girl said, extending her hand. "So hungry."

"Can you walk?"

She shook her head.

Fortunately, John inherited the strength and hardiness of his mother's side of the family. He managed to lift the girl into

The Last Slaughter

his arms, averting his eyes to avoid any unbecoming gaze upon her naked form, but also because of the rankness of her odor.

With his mother's lighter stowed away again, the darkness gathered unabated, and he found himself stumbling blindly, trying to locate the exit.

He felt her hot breath on his neck as he meandered through the hay.

"I know you," she said.

How could she possibly know him? How could she even see him? Maybe she'd developed exceptional night vision thanks to her imprisonment.

When he didn't answer, she said, "You'll feed me. No one's fed me in a long time, and I'm so, so hungry."

"I'll feed you," he said. "And we'll get you cleaned up."

Despite her unhygienic state, John's arousal only increased due to the oily warmth of her skin. His arms began to ache, and his knees started to wobble, despite how light she was. Clearly, Pinky Randall intended her to starve to death in that building.

Before his legs could surrender, he found the way out. More lightning illuminated the sky as they met the night air. John could breathe deeply again, his lungs filling with fresh air. Still carrying the girl, he hobbled toward the car, where he set her gently in the passenger seat. Though the car's interior light made her naked form starkly visible, he still buckled the seat belt for her and did his best not to touch her in a compromising way. "I'm sorry that I don't have a blanket or anything," he said.

She simply watched him with those big eyes of hers as he pressed buckle into place. He avoided returning her gaze, though he felt her continuing to watch him as he walked around the car to get behind the wheel.

The Last Slaughter

He paused with the door open, looking back toward the building. More lightning flashes, but still no rain. Nor, he well knew, would they see any.

"Wait here. Just a minute," he said to the girl sitting in the passenger seat.

As he walked back toward the building, he removed the lighter from his pocket. He kept looking back toward the car, making sure that the girl listened to what he said and didn't try to follow him or run away. He could see her still sitting there, her position unchanged. He continued to monitor her as he stepped up to one of the gasoline-soaked rags.

One more glance back to see her not only sitting there, but her head turned, watching him. He liked that. He wanted someone to see what he intended to do.

Then he lit the rag.

5

They spoke little as he drove, the long silences broken only when he tried to find out her name. She didn't seem to have one. Or she had many. The first time he asked, she muttered something he struggled to pronounce back to her. *Tonacacihautl,* she said, but his tongue tripped over the syllables. Then she said *AnnaKuori,* a name that sounded a little less foreign to his ears, but before he could repeat it, she added others. *Tari Pennu. Demeter.* He finally concluded that she suffered from some sort of delirium, or maybe she just wanted to fuck with him.

Behind them, the night lit up with an orange glow, the flames he set into motion now fully engulfing the building.

Trying to keep his eyes averted from her nudity, he considered her features, wondering if she crossed the border as a migrant worker. Maybe she feared he would turn her over to federal agents for deportation.

"I wouldn't do that," he said out loud without specifying what he meant.

Her eyes met his. Embarrassed, he returned his gaze to the road.

The Last Slaughter

"I mean I wouldn't hand you over to the authorities, if that's what you're worried about. Me and them don't get along too well. There's a certain deputy I hate, for one thing. I won't turn you over to Pinky Randall, either. We don't have an official sheriff, so he just acts like one, bossing everyone around. You can tell me your real name, if you want."

She reached over and touched his knee, causing him to flinch. He tried to concentrate on the driving. Something nagged at him. Did he forget something?

"Hungry," she said, but she didn't try to touch his knee again. She spoke softly, as if a prolonged period of silence made her vocal cords ache. "Starving."

"I know. I just need to get you someplace safe."

He counted on finding the deputy's car gone by the time he made it home, and he breathed a sigh of relief when he saw no sign of that mother-defiling idiot. Dawn began to break. Faintly, he smelled smoke, and that made him feel good. From somewhere far off he heard a siren. Maybe the deputy got called in to investigate the fire he set. He felt relieved that he had not set the building aflame with the girl inside it. That would have made him guilty of murder, a crime almost equal in weight to all the terrible things Pinky Randall had done, especially when you added human trafficking.

Still not knowing what to call her (*Tari? Demeter?*), he helped the girl out the car, wondering if she would ever come clean with him regarding her circumstances. Or if she would simply die. Severe hunger made her profoundly weak, but she seemed to have recovered the ability to walk at least, though he still had to assist her up the front steps and into the house. She paused at the threshold to look behind them at the dead pasture overlooking the home, visible now in the gloom of dawn. "My family used to farm here," he said. "A long time ago. Can't grow nothing here now. Not anymore. Everything's dried up and dead."

Whether or not that information made an impression, he couldn't tell. He wondered if he ought to clean her up before he tried to feed her, but once inside, she made the decision for him, hobbling to the kitchen table, bare-assed and filthy. What his mother would say if she found them like that, he could only imagine. He decided it didn't matter, so he began opening and closing cupboards, not surprised at all when he found little more than a bowl of sugar and a stale bread loaf. Even from a distance, the girl's odor proved strong, earthy and faintly metallic, like blood, but it no longer offended him. So he placed the bread and sugar in front of her and sat down in the adjacent chair.

At that moment, it hit him. What nagged him. What he'd forgotten.

"Goddammit," he said, and he struck the table with his fist.

The girl didn't react, though she watched him as he pressed his face into his hands. The bread and sugar sat untouched before her.

"I left the fucking tire iron," he said, finally. "I left it sitting there for them to find."

Rendered immobile by his own ineptness, he wondered if the flames would reach a temperature hot enough to melt iron. He doubted it.

Then he saw the way his table companion watched him, and the blankness of her expression infuriated him. Did she feel pity for him, or maybe he detected something mocking in those large eyes, almost too big for her face. Then he saw the food that sat ignored before her.

"I thought you were so goddamn hungry," he said. "Why the fuck don't you eat?" His voice sounded harsher than he intended, but she didn't so much as flinch, and somehow that

The Last Slaughter

made him angrier. He swept everything on the table to the floor, the bowl of sugar shattering to bits on the cheap linoleum. She regarded the mess on the floor with a neutral expression, as if observing a curious though unremarkable phenomenon.

Then she stood and walked out of the house.

For a moment, John just sat there, his fists clenched. How hot would it have to get for iron to melt? Still no clue. And what about the tires of the car? They left tracks, and he knew from the television that no longer worked how the authorities could match those to the car that made them.

Thoughts swirled in his head, and he almost didn't care where the girl had gone.

Then it mattered. He'd saved her, after all. At the very least, she owed him her silence.

He rushed out the door and saw her standing in the pasture. After making him carry her earlier, it turned out that she could move quite well. All an act, apparently.

He called out to her. "Hey!" But she didn't turn. Nor did she make an effort to run. She just stood there like a statue, a forgotten idol in a barren landscape, her form silhouetted in the growing light of morning.

As he made his way toward her, a peculiar feeling came over him, as if he'd stepped into the presence of something ethereal, eternal, transcendent. Maybe not those words exactly, but their ineluctable effects. His steps slowed as he came closer, the naked skin of her back glistening with perspiration.

Sensing his approach, she turned, and he saw that she held a shard taken from the broken sugar bowl. He reached for her, but she acted faster, taking his wrist and using the shard to slice into the palm of his hand.

He tried to wrench his hand away, but she held him firmly.

She twisted his wrist so that the blood dripped into the dust near their feet.

He stared at her in horror as her chapped lips formed a smile. "This is what I'm hungry for." Then she pressed his hand to her face, and he felt her tongue probing the wound, licking it. When she let his arm fall away, he saw his blood smearing her face. She smiled wickedly now, her teeth so white they looked predatory. "I know you," she said, repeating the words she muttered when he carried her to the car.

As they stood there in the desolation of the pasture, Laura stepped forth from the house. From a distance, she watched the two of them in silence.

6

Years ago, after her date with Pinky Randall changed her life forever, Laura struggled to care about anything. She barely finished school, ignoring assignments and homework, with one notable exception.

Hoping to instill an appreciation for how their community depended upon the food industry and the benevolence of Randall Meats, a teacher assigned Laura's class with a project to learn about traditions involving food. After all, Thanksgiving loomed on the horizon, and the teacher assumed that the students would write something nice about Pilgrims or Indians. But Laura surprised everyone by looking into something much more remote, unusual, and disturbing.

But Laura wrote her report on the *troksoi* system, a practice that affected people in faraway African nations like Togo and Ghana. Laura would never have learned about this system if not for a lonely girl who appeared at their school one morning, only to find herself instantly shunned by nearly everyone —except Laura, who felt like a pariah herself, if for different reasons. Besides, Laura thought it was stupid to dislike a person because of a dark complexion. Apparently in need of

The Last Slaughter

asylum, the new girl somehow found her way to their rural community, whether through clerical mistake or some act of official cruelty, no one knew. Either way, she faced endless bigotry and harassment, but that only made Laura more sympathetic.

From her new friend, Laura, learned about how under the *troksoi* system, female children as young as seven years old would be taken away from their families, usually to punish their parents for a crime like adultery. These children would lose their clothes, their selfhood, and even their name to become the wife of the gods. Forced to live inside a shrine, they would serve the priests of a deity such as *Nyigbla*. Such a deity would bless the community with bountiful food, but only after the sacrifice of the *troksoi*.

In her report, Laura wrote, "Offending these gods brings misfortune. If you expect them to give you food and wine, you need to offer them sacrifices, if not in blood then in isolation."

For her report, Laura received a D, her teacher noting that such things only happened in uncivilized places, and ought not Laura count her blessings that she lived in a place where people enjoyed the freedom to work for their own prosperity?

Now, as she sat in her own kitchen, Laura studied this girl found by John, this girl who seemed to have no proper name, and she recalled how she crumpled up that report and threw it in the trash. She wondered what became of that teacher in subsequent years. If she suffered some malady and became a human vegetable like her mother, Laura would not waste a single tear on her. If this was prosperity, Laura didn't want any more of it. And as for the classmate who told her about the *troksoi* system? She disappeared, simply failing to show up for school one day. Laura never learned if she was relocated or decided to run away on her own.

And she hadn't thought about her in years, but now she

wondered if John unwittingly rescued the victim of something similar—not in far off Ghana, but right here in their backyard.

But so far, the girl avoided answering their questions. She gazed back at John and Laura, her face indecipherable. Laura managed to get her covered with one of her mother's old bathrobes. Not that her nudity seemed to overly distract John, especially after that cutting episode. They managed to stop the bleeding, but Laura had to keep reminding him to keep his hand raised.

"Why exactly did you go into that godforsaken building?" she asked.

She listened as John told her again about how he just wanted another look at it. She still didn't understand why he went there without her. Then he added something he hadn't told her yet. "I heard her calling for help from inside."

"Calling for help, you say."

John didn't reply.

"So you can talk," said Laura to the mute girl. "If you can call out for help, you can say something to me."

A half-smile formed on the girl's lips. "I know you."

"That's what she said to me," said John.

"You know *me*? Or just him?" asked Laura. Distracted, John lowered his bleeding hand, and Laura brusquely raised it for him.

"I know you both," the girl said, still with that half-smile.

"You know us both *from where*? We don't know you at all."

No response, though the half-smile persisted. Laura sensed something uncanny in it, as if the girl really did know them, though from where, Laura had no idea. The fact that she came from that out-building that symbolized everything that had gone wrong with her life made Laura wary.

"Why were you there?" John started to answer, but Laura shushed him. "From your lips," she said to the girl.

The Last Slaughter

But before she could answer, someone knocked on the door with enough force that it shook in its frame.

"John Teecar," said the deputy from other side. "I'm here for you. And your mama ain't going to protect you this time."

John's hand fell again, but Laura didn't bother with lifting it this time. "What did you do?"

She stood before John could answer and headed for the door, not sure if she should open it or try to bar the deputy's way. The girl remained seated, her half-smile fixed and mocking.

Hesitating briefly, John removed his mother's lighter from his pocket and showed her, his face gone white.

"Oh, Jesus," she said. "Lock the door behind me." She opened the door, and before the deputy could react, she stepped through and shut it behind her. She prepared herself to feel the deputy's hands on her. She knew from the night before that he'd never heard of tenderness.

Instead, he rocked back on his heels, a hitch in his stance, like a regular Clint Eastwood. In one hand, he held a tire iron, and she wondered if he intended to use it to hammer down the door.

"Looks like you lost something," he said, gesturing with the crowbar.

Laura tried not to let her uncertainty show. She did her best to glower.

"Don't know what you're talking about. We don't own a crowbar."

He used it to point toward her car, which John left parked at a funny angle. "Came from there, I'm willing to bet. Your son used it to vandalize private property. Then he burned it to the ground."

Laura almost stopped herself from groaning out loud. "Not John. He was here all night."

The Last Slaughter

The deputy laughed and pretended to watch something in the distance. "Yeah, well, when I left, the car wasn't around. The call came in on the drive home, and my first thought was, 'Hmm, I wonder where that car went.' Left some clear tracks behind, too. Bet I could match them to those tires and not even worry about this." He lifted the crowbar and rested it on his shoulder, no longer Clint Eastwood and now Reggie Jackson.

Laura considered asking for it back if he didn't need it. She decided it best to wait out his silence with her own.

"The thing is," said the deputy, "Mr. Randall has a soft spot for you all. He's willing to overlook the destruction of his private property—on one condition." Once more, he gazed into the distance, and this time, he seemed to get lost in thought. Then his eyes lit up as if he noticed something for real this time. "You get yourself a hog?"

"What?" She truly had no idea what he meant, but she didn't want to step away from the door, suspecting a ruse to draw her away so that he could push his way inside. Their land had not supported any livestock in generations, and their finances had fallen so low that they couldn't afford the cost. If Walmart showed up to buy their property for a superstore, she wouldn't be able to sign the papers fast enough. But even they knew a dying community when they saw one.

The deputy shook his head. "Probably a wild boar. But I haven't seen one in years."

"Get on with what you were saying," said Laura.

Unaccustomed to commands from a woman, especially one who whored around, the deputy glowered. "Mr. Randall would like his property returned to him. John took something that belongs to him, and he wants it back. Return it, and he won't file charges. Pretty generous, if you ask me. Like I said, he has a soft spot for your family."

It took every ounce of control to keep herself rooted to her spot and not step away from the door to rip off the deputy's dick. She could not, however, stop what came out of her mouth. "Fuck you. Fuck him, too." Spittle flew from her mouth and clung to her chin. She did not wipe it away. If she did, the tears might follow, and she did not cry in front of anyone. Not anymore.

The deputy nodded. "Mr. Randall speculated you might say that. He might come out himself, and you'll hear all this straight from the horse's mouth."

After one more glance in the direction of the pasture, he got into his car and drove away.

Laura waited, making sure he left the driveway and made it to the main road. Then she stepped away from the door and looked toward what drew the deputy's attention.

She saw it—a pig, and a young one by the look of it, but still round in the belly. Well-fed and healthy, from what she could see. Its hide consisted of a pattern of brown and white fur. It hunkered over the spot where John and the girl stood not long before—by the looks of it, in the very place where the blood from John's hand fell. With its snout buried in the ground there, the pig fed heartily.

7

Moments afterwards, she and John would circle the animal carefully, each with a lassoed rope in their respective hands, careful so as not to scare it away. Perhaps because of its youth, the pig showed no concern over their approach, nor did it wander off as she feared it would when they went looking for rope.

It had taken work to motivate John to come out of the house. Through the window, he observed the exchange between her and the deputy, and he met her with lamentations when she returned inside.

"Quit sniveling and come out here with me," she said.

He denied sniveling, but Laura wouldn't have it. She didn't know when she would find it in her to forgive him for setting the fire, but that discussion would have to wait until they did something about the pig that wandered onto their property. His reaction to seeing it mirrored her own.

He said, "Could be others nearby, including its parents. I don't care to feel the wrath of a wild boar."

"Just find us some rope," said Laura. "Ought to be some in the shed."

The Last Slaughter

"What about her?" They'd left the girl sitting inside. After the deputy's visit, Laura only had more misgivings about what her son brought home, but she decided to keep them to herself for the time being. Something about the girl felt so wrong, and it gave her the heebie-jeebies when she said that she *knew* them.

"She's not going anywhere," Laura said, ignoring the premonition that came over her, the unsettling sense that they might eventually wish that she hadn't entered their lives in the first place.

John found the two coiled lengths of rope, barely eight feet long each, but they would have to do. Miraculously, the pig made no effort to evade them, remaining fixed to the spot of ground it had chosen to gorge upon. Apparently, something bloomed in the earth where John's blood spilled. The pig offered little objection when they led it away and tied it to an old fence post between the shed and the house. The whole thing struck them both as nothing short of miraculous.

Thinking of her conversation with the deputy, Laura said, "This animal follow you home from your little adventure?"

John shook his head, but his eyes looked faraway, lost in thought.

"Because," Laura said, "they think you stole something from your father."

"It's her," said John. "I rescued her. She was like you. A *prisoner.*"

That premonition again. "She's not like me. I wasn't a prisoner."

"We should name the pig," John said. "If we're going to keep it. I vote for Pinky."

She had to fight back the urge to slap him. She began to fret over how long they'd left the girl inside by herself. "Let's get back in," she said, and they left the pig alone and unnamed, but tethered at least, standing dumbly in the sun.

Inside, they found the girl's seat empty.

"Maybe she slipped out through a window," John said, and he marched toward the rear of the house, as if he planned to stop her from getting away. For a rare moment, Laura wondered if her son inherited some of his father's more unsavory characteristics. She shook it off, reminding herself that John mirrored her best self, that for all her limitations, she raised him correctly. Still, it made her uneasy to see him act so possessively of what did not belong to him. As he stood gazing out an open window, it dawned on Laura where the girl might have gone.

"Shut that window," she said. "She's in here."

They went to her mother's bedroom, where they found the girl sitting beside the catatonic woman.

Except that her mother now looked more awake and aware. Her eyes blinked around the room. They moved from the girl to Laura and then back to the girl. Her mouth twitched as if she intended to say something, but the muscles in her face would not obey her commands. The girl held the old woman's hand, which trembled as if it would reject the contact if it only had the strength.

The girl smiled at her and then at Laura.

"You like your gift?" the girl asked.

"Gift?" John's voice came from behind Laura. His eyes peered over her shoulder and into the room. She felt him wanting to get past her, but she remained in the doorway, barring his passage. He wanted the girl. Laura harbored no doubt about that.

"The animal," said the girl. "He's yours to have." Her big eyes sparkled. "I want the heart. You bring me the heart, and I'll bestow more."

The Last Slaughter

"More what?" Laura asked.

Instead of answering, the girl said, "You don't remember me, but I remember you. I thought that he brought you for me, a ripe, fertile, unsullied body. Then I smelled what you had in you. So I stayed back and watched as he took you for himself, right there in the hay. Then you ran away. And he left me there to starve."

Laura didn't speak. She couldn't find the words. She watched the girl's attention move away from her and toward her mother. The old woman looked like she would recoil if her body would only allow it, her gaze fixed with an expression of both wonder and horror as the girl stroked her hand.

"She acts like she doesn't know," said the girl to the older, stricken woman, "but you and I both do, and we know who put it in her. She still smelled so pretty and fresh, but I knew she wouldn't taste right, so I let her run away. I left it growing inside her."

Laura realized what she meant by *it*. John. She meant John.

"You get away from her." The words left Laura's mouth without her volition, the manifestation of rage that precedes reason and deceit. "You get away from all of us."

"You're not the first to live on this land," the girl said, "and you won't be the last. I've been with the first people, and I'll still be here when the sun finally gets tired and burns out. In the meantime, do what I say. Save the animal's blood, and bring me an offering. Its heart."

With her free hand, she opened the dying woman's nightgown, and she used a fingernail to draw a circle over the gray, mottled skin stretched like parchment over her sternum. Laura watched her mother's chest rise and fall quickly as the fingernail left behind an angry red mark, along with a spot of blood.

8

In defiance, they decided to let the pig escape. However, it demonstrated no inclination to run away. Even when they untied the rope from around its neck, it showed them no fear, merely sauntering back to the spot in the pasture where John's blood fell into the earth, once more burying its snout into the ground. Despite its feral appearance, it behaved like a contented, domesticated animal, a miracle if they ever saw one. They had no choice but to keep the animal, so once more they used the rope to tie it to the fence post. They watched it in silence as they pondered what they ought to do.

"What did she mean?" John finally asked.

Laura regarded him and pretended to not know what he meant.

"All that talk about smelling you. And someone putting something in you. I can barely say it." His mouth twisted as he spoke, his face like the one he made as a little boy when forced to drink cough syrup. Something inside her wanted to touch his face and wrap her arms around him, hugging him like a child she would never let go. "She's talking about Pinky Randall, right? She can't know about that."

The Last Slaughter

"She's making things up," Laura said. "She doesn't know what she's talking about."

John gestured toward the animal tied before them. It regarded them back, their indecision about its fate nothing more than a minor indisposition. "It's a good animal," said John. "Healthy. Got meat on its bones. I can't see us just letting it go."

No reply from Laura. She watched the animal watching them.

John couldn't wait out her silence. "I say we let her have its heart. She's just crazy, so what hurt would it do? Is that what you think, too?"

Now she turned to him. "Do I think what?"

"That she's crazy." He tried smiling at her, but the effort only made him look like his father, and for the first time, Laura felt afraid of him. She studied his features, looking for signs of Pinky Randall in her son.

"She's something. Find a good metal bucket and take him to the shed. Do what she said. Make sure you catch all its blood."

"All of it?"

"Just do like she said. You know how to cut it."

"It's in my DNA," John said. Without another word, he took the animal's rope. "Come along, Pinky," he said as he led the pig away.

Laura watched them go, wincing at the name.

9

The animal remained pliant, giving John no trouble. Not only did it allow John to lead it to the shed, but it offered no resistance when he tied together its back feet. Soon, John had it suspended upside down. It hardly grunted, and when John used a knife to slice its thick neck, it shuddered but did not squeal. John cursed himself when he realized he didn't have the bucket positioned properly, and some of the blood spilled onto the planks of the floor.

Once he bled the hog dry, John began making the cuts down the center so that he could strip it of its hide. Though unpracticed, he managed to remove it without too much mess, and from there, he used the knife to saw away the skin from the meat. He acted on instinct rather than experience, and he surprised himself by doing a good job. John imagined the ghost of his grandfather whispering instructions to him, and for all he knew, the old man's spirit inhabited him and worked through him for the duration of the process. This thought gave him pleasure, and in time he began to enjoy himself, even whistling by the time it came time to gut the hog. Only

The Last Slaughter

when he had the animal washed down the meat hanging from hooks did he remember to save the heart. He nearly fumbled it, his hands so wet with gore and viscera, so he set it inside the bucket of blood for good safe keeping. Then he returned to the house.

He saw the girl waiting for him outside. He felt a flutter in his chest at the sight of her wearing a t-shirt that belonged to his mother, reaching just far enough to cover her thatch of pubic hair. In his imagination, he saw himself married to her and wondered what she would do if he tried to kiss her.

But she paid him little mind other than to ask, "Where is it?"

He faced the reality that the hunger in her eyes was not for him. He indicated the bucket that swung from his hand, the animal's gore slopping onto the ground. She took it greedily and plunged her hands into it. Out they came with the heart of the beast. He watched as she sat back onto her haunches and bit into it.

John didn't know what he expected. Perhaps he didn't imagine she would cook it, but the sight of her devouring the raw organ left him frozen. When she finished, she smiled at him, her front covered with blood, bits of tissue between her teeth. Surprisingly, his romantic notions did not flee at the sight of her mastication, and part of him still wanted to kiss her.

"You don't have to eat that," he said, doing his upmost to mask his disgust. "Plenty of meat off the carcass."

She paused to wipe her mouth with the back of her arm. Then she used the same blood-smeared arm to point at the bucket. "Take that to the spot where I bled you. Pour it into the earth. I'll bestow more. That'll be my gift."

"What the fuck are you?"

"Just do it and witness for yourself. I'll call forth a flock of chickens. How does that sound?"

He laughed and looked up at the clouds. "Tasty. Why not a cow?"

"You want a whole cow, do you? One you can eat all by yourself?"

John believed he could in fact eat a whole cow by himself. With things becoming scarce, they'd gone so long with so little that he no longer knew what counted as gluttony.

He left her sitting on her haunches, blood-smeared and devouring the remainder of her meal. Once in the pasture, it took him little effort to identify the spot she meant. Tiny flowers sprung up there, and he considered plucking them from the earth and presenting them to her as a gift. Maybe slick his hair back and see if one of his grandfather's button-down shirts fit him. But instead, he followed her instructions, upending the bucket and letting the blood cover the flowers and seep into the ground.

Once he completed the process, he turned to see if he earned the girl's approval. But she no longer sat there.

Instead, he saw the deputy leaning against his vehicle, watching him.

"What you got there, John?" the deputy asked as John returned with the bucket. "That looked like an awful lot of blood."

The bucket's handle felt hot in John's hand. He wondered if he could swing it with enough force to crack the deputy's skull. At least knock him unconscious for a while.

The deputy must have sensed these thoughts because he touched his service pistol as John came closer.

"You housing livestock?" the deputy asked.

John didn't break his stride as he continued to close the

The Last Slaughter

distance between them. The deputy walked to the other side of the car, trying to make the move look casual. John continued his march toward the shed.

"If you're harvesting livestock, I need to know," the deputy said.

John stopped and tried to lock eyes with the deputy, but the man's sunglasses made it impossible.

"There a law I'm breaking?" said John.

"It's a local industry. You're stealing from people's livelihoods."

John tried to laugh out loud at this remark, but the sound that existed his throat sounded like a groan—a weak one even to his own ears.

"You ready to return Mr. Randall's property?" asked the deputy as John continued past him toward the shed, no more caution in his voice, apparently certain now that John would not try to bash him in the head.

Only John didn't share the man's confidence. Aware that he shouldn't open the door in the man's presence, he stopped, but he didn't have a chance to answer.

His mother did that for him.

"If Pinky Randall lost something, he can go look for it elsewhere," she said. "Or he can go fuck himself. Tell him I don't much care which."

Turning, the deputy smiled at her. John wondered how many strikes with the metal bucket it would take to see the man's skull. An old commercial jingle ran through his mind.

"You can tell him yourself," the deputy said. "He said no way can you say no to him. He said you don't know the meaning of the word."

"Time to leave, Gerald," said Laura.

John didn't even realize the deputy had a name, and it goaded him to hear his mother use it.

"I almost told Mr. Randall I already knew you couldn't say no, but I thought I ought to keep that as our little secret. A gentleman doesn't talk."

"Go on now," Laura said. "Don't come back."

"Where is that pig I saw earlier? You already slaughter it?" Scanning the area, his eyes fell on the figure who appeared in the doorway to the house—the girl, still wearing a shirt without britches. "Well, hello there. Seems I won't have to send Mr. Randall after all."

He stepped forward, clearly intending to clear a path to the door by pushing Laura aside.

Only he didn't make it far.

John moved faster than the deputy (*Gerald*, he told himself), and with a mighty swing of the bucket, he sent the officer sprawling face first. His victim wore no hat, and from his head erupted a plume of blood. John leaned over and struck him again. In his mind, that old jingle continued to play on repeat. *How many licks does it take...?*

Not two, apparently. John struck a third time.

Though senseless, the law man had not fallen unconscious. He managed to roll over and look at John in mute terror. One of his eyes began filling with blood.

"How many licks does it take?" John said along with the voice in his head, but nothing could drown out his mother, who screamed for him to stop. But he struck again, this time aiming for the deputy's face.

When John lifted the improvised weapon, the deputy's nose appeared comically smaller, reduced to crushed bone and cartilage. Drool flowed from his half-open lips along with tooth fragments. The blood eye came dislodged and lay against his cheek, holding on by a sliver of optic nerve. A horrible gurgling noise arose from the man's throat as he choked on blood and the remains of his teeth.

The Last Slaughter

"Not four licks, that's for sure," John told the voice in his head. "Maybe five?" He may have spoken out loud, but he wasn't sure.

For good measure, he brought down the bucket two more times.

10

Laura would never unsee her sweet boy obliterating the deputy's face. The vision would haunt her dreams, and during her waking moments, nothing could hold her attention long enough before she squeezed her eyes shut and physically shuddered. Nothing could blot it out, and she could hear that noise he made while inflicting violence. Was he singing? She felt certain she heard him singing as he turned the man's face to pulp. Almost as worse, the sight of her own flesh and blood with that wide-eyed stared, standing over the deputy's immobile form when it finally stopped. She wanted to run away screaming, and it took everything inside her to resist that impulse.

"Give it to me, John," she said afterwards, her voice barely above a whisper. He didn't respond, instead clinging to the bucket as he loomed over the deputy, his breath haggard and heavy.

Only when she gently took the bucket out of John's hand did she realize that the sound of breathing came from the deputy. John barely made a sound, but he released the bucket.

The Last Slaughter

Together, they watched the deputy, her thoughts scrambling over what they ought to do with him, his thoughts indecipherable. Surely, the deputy wouldn't live that much longer, would he? He'd lost both of his eyes, and his nose rammed into his face, Laura didn't know how he could go on breathing. For his sake, she hoped he'd fallen unconscious and could feel nothing, but some part of his brain obviously refused to give up. She noticed that his left hand trembled near his holster, as if he wanted to locate his gun. She considered taking it herself and shooting him.

Before she could act on this impulse, the girl stepped forth from the house.

"Take him into the shed," she said. The command in her voice told Laura that she'd watched the whole thing. "Find a blanket and wrap it around him so he can stay warm."

At first, Laura misunderstood and took her to mean that she intended to nurse the deputy back to health. John obeyed and began dragging the man by his feet. Then the meaning became clear: she wanted to keep the man's circulatory system going for a little while longer. She wanted a warm heart to bite into.

As John completed his task, Laura found herself unable to move. Frozen, she looked at the deputy's car, struggling to come to terms with the fact that they needed to do something about its presence.

She hadn't noticed the flock of hens that gathered in the pasture, their beaks poking at the spot where the pig once rooted. Whatever called forth the swine now called forth the fowl. Laura felt the girl watching her in expectation. For what, she didn't know. Thanks? Praise? Laura could only provide hatred and fear.

"You can keep them for their eggs. Slaughter them now or

when they go barren. They'll provide a bounty as long as you keep feeding me," the girl said.

"I ought to kill you." Trembling, Laura could barely form the words.

The girl responded with a chilling smile. She returned to the house as if she owned it. Laura didn't stop her.

11

The girl liked the old woman, her quiet, her warmth. She liked how she could press her body against hers and listen to her heartbeat. She noticed a slight arrhythmia, but she could tell the woman possessed an otherwise strong heart. It responded to her presence by growing more rapid, as if it wanted to leap out of the woman's chest and into her mouth.

"You smell so good," she whispered, curling herself into a fetal position alongside her.

She wondered what this woman would say if the stroke had not robbed her of speech. The blood coursing through her body would have to communicate for her, the veins and arteries swelling and stretching with the rise of blood pressure. Another stroke would finish her for good, so she stroked the woman's chest and cooed for her to breathe more evenly.

She'd taken the form of an elderly woman many times before, crow-faced and wrinkled, offering spells in exchange for gifts. On this land once lived a people who trusted her, saw her age not as infirmity, but as a sign of great wisdom. They knew how to honor her, and their sacrifices came to her willingly, bestowed with ornamental jewelry, and she would

The Last Slaughter

sometimes huddle with these sacrifices inside huts made from wood and stone, much like she now did on this bed made for dying, while outside the others danced and celebrated the coming harvest. She experienced true happiness those days, not like now, when the greed of men led to such unflattering treatment.

How long had she been held prisoner? Enough time for her to grow weak with hunger, but now she felt her strength returning. In no time, the mother and her son would let go of their misgivings about her, and they would come to appreciate the bountiful blessings she could provide. No doubt they would enjoy the hens as well as the swine, and she would provide more. Corn once grew on this land, rows and rows of it, and the people ate it and sang songs to her. She answered by providing abundance. In lakes and rivers, now dried up and vanished, she summoned fish to leap into their boats, and everyone was happy.

She thought of the man's heart and how good it would taste. She would reward this offering with a cow. Perhaps two. Later, she would teach them the songs once sung in her glory, though she herself struggled to remember them clearly. Maybe they could invent their own. It didn't matter. Just as long as they provided her with offerings.

Her thoughts wandered as she used a fingernail to trace the circle she created earlier on the old woman's sternum. She would never allow anyone to misuse her or her gifts again. She was meant to feel the sun's rays or stand in fields of dirt as rain fell and soaked the earth. She liked to feel the stirring of growth beneath her feet.

She must have pressed too deeply into the groove of the old woman's flesh, for a trickle of blood appeared. "I'm sorry," she said to the woman who trembled wordlessly against her. She licked her finger clean, then used her tongue on the space between the woman's withered breasts. With the coppery scent came another memory: seeing the younger version of Laura brought into her dungeon by her jailer. She supposed he never intended to feed her, for that moment marked the beginning of her starvation. Instead, he wanted to show her the power he held over her, making her observe the spectacle from the shadows. Indeed, she watched with curiosity as Laura fought and struggled against her assailant. At the time, he still fed her on occasion, and she listened to the beating of their hearts in anticipation of a feast. But she noticed something else too, not quite an additional heartbeat, not yet at least. More like the echo of one from some future place. She realized then that something already grew in that womb her jailer sought to violate, something small, newly formed and barely stirring. Already inclined to reject this meal if he offered it to her, she quietly rejoiced when the girl successfully fought him, kicking him in his naked groin and causing him to curl into a moaning ball of pain. As she watched the girl escape with her dress torn, her face bruised and bleeding, she wondered if she already knew what she carried in her womb.

"Did you know?" She whispered the question to the stricken woman whose bed she now shared. The body next to her shuddered in reply.

She obviously did know, and the girl pondered what a terrible thing that was. An awful secret. She could practically read this elderly mind and see for herself those late nights spent alone in that recliner. Father and daughter. Under this very roof.

Like her, Laura must have felt like a prisoner. Such unexpected ways their destinies intertwined.

The girl broke more skin, this time deliberately, and more blood appeared. She did so without apology.

After this humiliation, her jailer stopped bringing her

offerings. In response, the land went into decline. With magical glyphs he learned from his father (who learned them from his own), he kept her bound in that place, until she assumed he'd forgotten all about her. There, she grew hungry and became nostalgic for the songs once sung in her honor.

"I wish you could sing to me," she whispered to the woman, whose heat kept her warm. Again, she heard the heart flutter and felt the body tremble. "Maybe," she said, an idea coming to her, "you can pay your tribute in other ways."

12

The deputy somehow went on breathing, just refusing to die. At one point, Laura prepared a bowl full of broth and brought it to him in the shed, where he lay in the corner underneath a blanket, just as the strange girl instructed. Laura wanted to call for help, but she knew what they would do to John, so she just prayed for the deputy to finally die. Instead, he stubbornly clung to life.

Laura couldn't see how. She tried to feed him the broth with a spoon, but the effort only resulted in a mess. He hardly had a functioning mouth anymore, not after what happened to his jaw under the blows of the bucket.

After nearly giving up, Laura thought she could hear words come out of his mouth. It unnerved her to do so, but she moved her ear closer to where his tongue dangled.

Not talking, she realized. Humming. He was trying to sing.

Laura tried to guess the tune, but she couldn't place it. If she could recognize it, then maybe she could sing it back to him and provide some modicum of comfort. She hoped he made these sounds in a state of unconsciousness, if not sleep, then some approximation of it. How much function remained

The Last Slaughter

in his brain, she couldn't guess, but she hoped that the world to him now amounted to a pleasant low-fi dream. Maybe one in which he replayed a song once sung to him by his mother. She tried to match the tune by humming. She never could sing. Whenever she tried to sing to John, he would just cry and cry, so she stopped altogether. Now she tried to sing the deputy (*Gerald*, she reminded herself) into the next world.

Moments later, the girl appeared in the entryway, followed by John. John's hand once more gripped that notorious bucket. Without saying anything to her, he stepped into the shed and began using the bucket to collect the eggs from the chickens now roosting there.

"You can go on," said the girl. She meant the singing. Laura stopped when the others appeared. "Or I can teach you a different song." The girl looked at John, who blushed and went about collecting the eggs, pretending not to hear. "I can teach you both."

"If we sing," Laura said, "will you go away?"

The deputy's distorted song became a gurgle. Once more, Laura shuddered to imagine how much awareness of his surroundings he maintained.

"It's time to get the knife," the girl said to John.

Carefully, so as not to break the eggs, John set the bucket on the floor planks. Laura could sense him hesitating, his eyes daring back and forth between her and the girl.

"Leave it be, John," Laura said. She felt no more aversion to touching the deputy. She pulled him close, keeping his head cradled on her lap. "Nobody's harming this man any further."

John appeared undecided, but his eyes roamed the shed. Roosting on a pile of straw, the hens clucked softly, like a Greek chorus watching events unfold.

"I don't see it," he said.

With those words, Laura's hopes that her son felt some moral ambivalence began to fade.

She was glad she'd hidden the knife.

The girl studied her face in a knowing way. "Don't you like what I've given you? Meat. Fresh eggs."

"You didn't give us these things." Spittle flew from Laura's mouth as she spoke. "You're an abomination. I don't know what you are. Why don't you just leave?"

"You give me what I want," the girl said, "and I'll bestow other gifts. A cow. Would you like that?"

Ignoring them, John lumbered about the shed. He upended a tub of old rags, then a crate filled with ancient paint containers. Biting her lip, Laura watched him. The girl studied her expression. Then as if reading Laura's thoughts, she pointed to a corner. "Under there," she said.

Laura could feel the heat emanating from the deputy's forehead. He began to sing again, and the girl swayed to the melody. John went to the corner and lifted an old gas can. "Found it," he said, lifting the knife from its hiding place.

Crying, Laura tried to ward John away by waving her hand. He paused in his approach, as if waiting for her to say something. When no words materialized, he said, "A cow, Mama. She's going to bring us a *cow*."

Then he straddled the deputy's prone body, and as Laura held the dying man's head, he began cutting out his heart.

13

The promise of a cow came fulfilled.

The girl ate the deputy's heart in front of them without shame or embarrassment, and afterwards, she instructed them to bury the rest of the body in the pasture, specifying the spot where the other blood fell. John worked by himself into the evening digging the hole, and after filling the earth atop the deputy, he ate a robust meal and eventually fell into a deep sleep.

Before alighting to bed, he told his mother goodnight and professed his love for her, but she said nothing back to him. She seemed disinclined to talk to him anymore, a turn of events he could not have foreseen, especially considering how she'd made him her confidante throughout his life. Even before he could form complete sentences, she would tell him about the misfortunes that befell them, all thanks to that confounded Pinky Randall.

For that reason, he didn't know what to think when he caught his mother singing to that fuckwit deputy (*Gerald*—how he hated that name). The sight of her doing that made him feel like an intruder, and before falling asleep, he tried to recall even one instance where she'd sung to him. Considering he remembered every conversation between them, he doubted she'd ever had done anything like that for him. If he couldn't remember it, it didn't happen. Maybe he didn't possess the highest IQ in the world, but he possessed an unparalleled memory, not counting occasions like leaving behind a tire iron after an act of arson.

These troubling thoughts managed to leave his sleep undisturbed. That night, he dreamed vividly. Some strange shit, too, mostly about the girl. He'd seen her undressed, and he didn't dare touch her, but not so in dreams. There, in the pasture, they laid with one another in his dream, her on top, her pelvis grinding into his. At some point in the dream, he became distracted by a circle of onlookers, men and women with strange clothes and features, all of them singing in a language he couldn't understand. The girl paid them no mind, and after a moment, neither did he. But before they could complete their carnal act, his body began to decay. Soon, he couldn't move, and he relied on her to maintain the rhythm of their coitus. Eventually, his flesh rotted away completely, and only his bones remained. The girl continued to grind until even the bones became dust that dispersed in the wind.

He awoke feeling as if he had not slept at all. Even more hungry than restless, he heard his stomach growl, so he scrambled himself three eggs and he fried bacon. He couldn't think of another time in his life when he could afford himself such a luxury. Hoping the aroma of cooking would attract his mother, he scrambled another egg after wolfing down his first breakfast. When she didn't appear, he ate it himself as he stood near the window. There, he gazed toward the pasture, where he saw it, just like she promised.

A cow.

He smiled and took his time eating, confident he could

approach the animal on his own time without fear of scaring it off, just like the others. He washed his plate, scrubbing it completely clean before going off to find a coil of rope. Maybe they would have fresh milk soon. He couldn't see how his mother could go on mourning the deputy when such luxuries waited for them on the horizon.

Surprisingly, the cow did resist him, tossing its neck and running before he could get close enough. His hands fumbled with the rope, too, and despite such a grand beginning to a beautiful morning, he became frustrated. He swore at the cow, as if unkind words would make it stand still.

"Ain't much of a cowboy, I see."

John twisted around at the sound of the voice. He found himself staring at Pinky Randall standing within a few feet of him.

He'd seen Pinky Randall plenty of times, but always at a distance, never this close. Nor had Pinky Randall ever acknowledged his existence before. Seeing him now, so close, caused John to stop his struggles with the cow. Dumbfounded, he stared at his father, who wanted nothing to do with him, and he found himself cataloguing the flaws and imperfections in the man's appearance: the balding head badly disguised with a comb-over, the full belly hanging over the belt loops of his jeans. Such flaws made John realize that despite his justifiable hatred of this man, he had elevated him to a god-like status in his imagination. It took all his inner strength not to kneel in supplication. Something brown marred the side of Pinky Randall's nose, some kind of mole, perhaps even cancerous. How could a man with such grotesque features accrue so much wealth and power? Of course, John knew Pinky inherited everything that belonged to him, and he felt renewed resentment over how those things would never get passed down to him. His lawful birthright. He stood there, hating and worshipping Pinky Randall all at the same time, as if the deity of an unjust existence had just come down from the heavens and stood before him. It dawned on him for the first time that his mother had not only taught him to hate Pinky Randall, but also fear him at the same time.

"Judging by the look of things around here," said Pinky Randall, "I need look no further for what has been taken from me."

The girl, thought John, *he knows she's here.* But he reached deep down into his hatred and drew forth defiance. "I ain't got nothing that belongs to you. I wouldn't *want* what you've got."

Pinky laughed, as if he'd just heard a good one.

"I'm just a businessman who's trying to protect his property. I take it you've got a mind for business, too?"

Wary of trap, John didn't answer.

Pinky sniffed, his eyes scanning the area. "I was going to ask what happened to Deputy Purvis. Judging by the presence of livestock, I don't expect him to be clocking in and reporting for work any time soon."

"No one's seen him," John said. "Couldn't say when or if he'll show up anywhere. If he doesn't, maybe we can get a proper sheriff in this town."

Pinky erupted with laughter. "Boy, you've got a mouth on you. Do you even know who I am?"

John nodded, feeling again that sense of standing in the presence of a deity and hating himself for it. He wondered if the laughter might wake up the rest of the house.

"The people here don't need a sheriff. They have me. I am the law. And that means I can overlook Deputy Purvis' mysterious disappearance." He winked at John's feet and the freshly dug earth of the grave beneath them. "And you're going to need a lot more to keep this up. Once you start, she wants more and more and more. Pretty soon, it gets tiring."

The Last Slaughter

No longer harassed by John, the cow stood still, grazing upon a clump of weeds. Pinky walked toward it, and John noted that the animal didn't run this time, remaining in place and even allowing Pinky to pet it behind its ears. The cow's udders hung heavy and full between its legs, and it seemed to listen as Pinky whispered something to it. Then Pinky removed something from the belt around his waist, something which the overhanging flesh hid from view.

"I could teach you to cowboy," Pinky said. "But as a businessman yourself, I'm sure you understand how rivalry works."

John now saw what he held. A pistol, its barrel pressed to the animal's head. John cried out, and Pinky wavered, turning the pistol in John's direction as if anticipating violence. Instead, he smiled. "Why, hello Laura."

John's mother marched toward them, her mouth stretched as if in preparation of a terrible scream. Her steps slowed when she saw the gun, but her approach continued.

"It's been a long time," said Pinky.

"You need to leave now," she said.

Pinky looked at John. "Which one of you hid Deputy Purvis' vehicle?"

John spoke softly, the words nearly caught in his throat. "She did."

Pinky returned his attention to Laura, who now stood next to John. "Well, that was a piss-poor job. Not far from here, hidden behind a few trees. Did you *want* your son to get caught, Laura?"

John turned to her, curious to hear the answer. He wondered if he did the wise thing in letting her take care of the car while he disposed of the remains.

"He's *your* son," Laura said, evidently not inclined to

answer the real question. John wondered: *did* she want him to get caught and perhaps wind up on Death Row?

Another bellowing round of laughter from Pinky, this time with more contempt. "I don't think so," he said once he could get enough air. To John, he added, "You haven't swallowed that load of horse shit, have you?"

"I don't know," said John. He found himself withering under Pinky's gaze, and he believed him. "No. I don't believe it."

"John," said Laura.

John waited for more, but she had nothing to add.

"Alright, then," Pinky said. "Listen, cowboy, you keep salt inside that house?"

John thought about it. Then he nodded.

"A lot of it?"

John shook his head.

"Well, we're going to need a lot of it, because you're going to salt this earth. All of it. And I'm going to come back and make sure you did it." He lifted the pistol, and for a moment, John thought he planned on shooting his mother. He tried to position himself to shield her, but it turned out that Pinky had other ideas.

With methodical precision, he placed the barrel between the cow's eyes and shot it dead.

They all watched it shudder once before its legs folded, causing it to fall to the earth.

"You'll want to bury that first," Pinky said, still gripping the pistol.

John watched as heat rose like steam from the expiring animal. The shot still ringing in his ears, he finally dropped to his knees, but he did so in order to press his head against its hide, hoping to conceal his tears. He also wanted to listen for signs of life within the cow, wondering if he could use his cutting skills to rescue a calf in its womb before it died, too.

But he heard nothing. Instead he felt Pinky's hand on his back. "There, there," Pinky Randall said. "Stand up like a man. Not just for your mother, but for your grandmother, too. I see the gunshot has roused her from the house."

Confused, John looked up and saw his grandmother approaching them.

Laura saw, too. Her mouth hung open in a struggle to put disbelief into words. The woman had shown no signs of recovery and had not walked in years, but she appeared strong in her bearing, her face no longer showing the effects of the stroke that debilitated her.

"Gracey, it has been a long time," Pinky Randall said. "I've not seen you since Ralph's funeral. I heard that you weren't well, so it's a pleasure to see you looking so spry."

He let his arms hang at his side, as if he anticipated a hug from the woman who did answer or break her stride. Instead, Gracey walked past him and knelt next to John. She placed her hand on the cow and looked at John.

"There will be another one. You watch and see," she said, her voice barely worn around the edges, not at all like that of a woman unused to speaking.

John studied her face through the tears that marred his vision. He struggled to remember how she looked and sounded before the stroke. Not like the woman he saw now. He could recall that much. Her eyes looked big and dark, unmarred by cataracts or any other sign of age.

"Gracey," said Pinky Randall, "there's evidently some controversy regarding the paternity of this young man. Perhaps you can put the boy's mind to rest. Am I his father?"

Still regarding John, his grandmother said, "No."

"There you have it," said Pinky. "Laura, even your own mother says you're a liar."

"Goddamn you," said Laura, quietly at first, as if speaking to herself, but then she repeated the words loud enough for all the heavens to hear. That seemed to open the floodgates of repressed rage, and with each word she spoke to her mother, her voice rose in volume, eventually growing as loud as thunder. "You let it happen. You knew it was happening. *You just did nothing.*"

The final sound that escaped her throat came out as a sob, and John thought she'd exhausted her rage. But then Laura fell upon the old woman, biting, tearing, clawing. His grandmother did not fight back, either from surprise or because she'd resolved to let her own daughter tear her apart. Someone laughed, probably Pinky Randall, though John couldn't swear that the laughter didn't come from himself. His own actions seemed to occur without his volition.

Like grabbing the gun from Pinky. Or maybe Pinky handed it to him. He couldn't remember. He could hardly recall firing it three times.

The first shot hit his mother in the back. She turned, looking at him with an expression of surprise and betrayal. Or maybe she didn't recognize him. Whatever the case, John barely recognized himself anymore. He liked to think that his finger just slipped the second time, when the bullet hit her shoulder. She held up her good arm, like she intended to reach out to him. She took one step in his direction, but the third shot ripped through her skull, and she dropped like a sack of potatoes.

"I would bury her over here, too," said Pinky Randall, "and I highly recommend you do it *before* you salt the earth."

The vision of his mother went blurry, and only after a moment did John realize that was because he was crying. He felt Pinky Randall take the pistol from his hand, and he offered no resistance.

Once more, Pinky patted him on the shoulder, but it brought no consolation. "I do want what belongs to me. I expect she's in the house."

John and his grandmother followed Pinky toward the entrance. As they passed the shed and heard the sound of the chickens, Pinky instructed him that they would all have to be destroyed, too, along with any eggs they left behind. The man walked ahead of them without fear, arms swinging in confidence that John either would not or could not inflict any harm upon him. Eventually, they came to the grandmother's room, and if Pinky demonstrated no surprise at what they found, other than to say, "Well, I'll be."

The girl's body appeared mummified, its brown flesh brittle and flaking. It huddled there in the middle of the bed, legs pulled up in a fetal position, one thumb in its mouth as if it tried to suckle before it died. From all appearances, that death occurred a millennia ago. John babbled something, as if someone compelled him to explain the impossible. Pinky told him to shut up. John's grandmother stood behind them both, observing.

"Well, good riddance," Pinky said. "This goes in the hole, too. Show me where you keep the salt. You're going to need a lot of it."

14

As it happened, John did not own enough salt to get the job done, so Pinky explained that he would return later with what they needed. "You killed the only man I trusted," Pinky said, "so you're going to have to do all this work by yourself. I'll expect you not to tax your grandmother by making her assist you in any way. The good woman has been through enough in her lifetime."

Pinky paused, observing the effect of this speech on John's grandmother. If he expected praise or thanks or an offer of iced tea, he received none of these things. If, like John, he noticed something strange about her eyes, he gave no indication of that either. The two of them watched mutely as Pinky pulled his bulk into his pink convertible. Before driving away, Pinky pointed his finger at John. "I want that hole completed before I get back later. Everything done the way I told you. You hear me?"

John didn't answer. He just stared at this man he once thought of as his distant father.

Still, Pinky nodded as if John said something that met his approval. "You do a good job, and I'll give you a job. There's an opening, I hear. Maybe you'll make deputy eventually." And then he roared away in a cloud of dust.

John spent the rest of the morning digging. Not surprisingly, he struggled over how to move the cadaver of the cow. Eventually, he got the idea of using the rope to tie it to the bumper of the car and using that to move it, but he only succeeded in pulling off the bumper. Exhausted and barren of ideas, he sat on the ground next to his mother's corpse and once more began to cry. After some time of that, he looked up to discover his grandmother watching.

"I expect that you'll be asking for her heart," John said.

His grandmother smiled. "No. She's been through too much. She gets to keep her heart."

John nodded and wiped away his tears. He wanted to take it back, take everything back. Later, when he finished his task, he would take his grandmother to the site of Ralph Teecar's burial site, and he would smash that lying grave marker in front of her. He would reduce it to rubble. He might even piss on the grave. He would tell her all the facts about his existence that he'd put together in just that little while, but he suspected she already somehow knew.

Giving up on the cow for the time being, he went inside the house and carried the mummified corpse of the girl outside. Bits of her came apart during the process, and it took him more time than he expected to make sure he got everything. He carried the body to the hole, cradled like a baby. Behind him, his grandmother followed, carrying a foot that fell off some distance back. Delicately, so as not to disturb any more of her remains, he lifted the body into the hole. Then he did the same to his mother, positioning the bodies so that they lay side by side. Afterwards, he looked down upon his work, wondering if he ought to say something.

Standing next to him, his grandmother spoke instead.

"I am hungry, though," she said. "Starving, in fact."

He nodded. He knew what she liked to eat. He marked the hour and calculated how long it might take for Pinky Randall to return with his supplies. He thought of how he bled the hog suspended by his ankles, and he thought of how the same process should work just fine again. One last slaughter, he thought.

Then his grandmother said, "I'll bestow plenty more gifts after that."

Okay, he decided, maybe not the very last.

THE END

ABOUT THE AUTHOR

Douglas Ford's short fiction has appeared in a variety of anthologies, magazines, and podcasts, as well as two collections (*Ape in the Ring and Other Tales of the Macabre and Uncanny* and *The Infection Party and Other Stories of Dis-Ease*). His longer works include *The Beasts of Vissaria County*, *Little Lugosi (A Love Story)*, *Babble*, and most recently, *The Trick*. He lives on the west coast of Florida.

ALSO BY DOUGLAS FORD

The Beasts of Vissaria County

Little Lugosi: A Love Story

The Reattachment

The Infection Party and Other Stories of Dis-ease

Ape in the Ring & Other Tales of the Macabre and Uncanny

A Tale in the Barroom Gothic

CAT FOOD

by Holly Rae Garcia

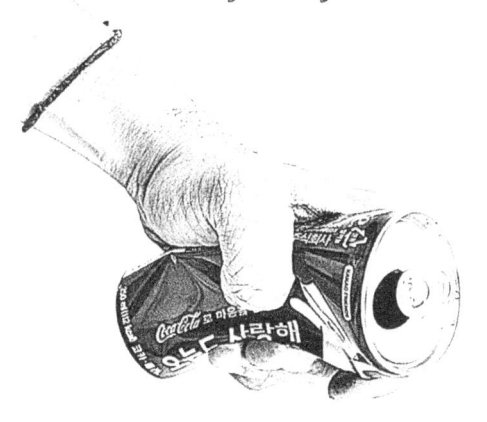

For Maggie

1

Jason's bare feet shuffled against the carpet as he crept down the narrow hallway. Holding his flip-flops in one hand, he paused at the door to his dad and stepmom's room. Moving closer, he held his breath and put his ear against the door. He didn't know why he tip-toed or bothered to check on them; he could have set his watch to their nighttime routine. Once the door closed, their joint snoring vibrated halfway across the house within ten minutes. But that night had been different, *important*, and he wanted to make sure they were out, but not *too* out. He didn't know exactly how many sleeping pills to slip into their sweet tea at dinner that evening, and he had erred on the side of a permanent coma over not quite asleep. It wouldn't be any great personal loss to him if they never woke up, the two of them deserved that and more. He'd probably have to get his own place and ask for more hours at the restaurant, but Lou was always bugging him to pick up shifts so that wouldn't be an issue.

Jason sighed with relief and continued down the hallway. The snoring didn't seem quite as loud as usual, but he was pretty sure they were both snoring. He didn't *hate* them, after

Cat Food

all. More like an extreme aversion to their very existence. He did, however, hate the idea of going to prison so all in all he figured it was okay that they were still alive.

He stopped at the narrow table near the front door and grabbed his keys. He froze as they clinked against the glass top, but nothing stirred besides Bertha, their orange and white cat. She sashayed out of the kitchen and wound herself around his legs, purring. Jason reached down and scratched behind her ears before opening the door to the garage.

"Stay here," he whispered to Bertha, though she hadn't obeyed a single thing in her ten years of life so he wasn't sure why he ever talked to her at all.

Back when things were still getting built around town, he had stolen a box of thick construction trash bags and hidden them in a blue plastic bin in their garage. At the time, he wasn't sure what he would need them for but his buddy Sam had said to grab them, so he did. Jason walked to the corner of the garage, the concrete cool against his bare feet. He stepped over a stack of old fence posts his dad had saved to use in the burn pit. Jason leaned down and removed the cracked plastic lid from the tub. He pulled the bags from the bin, barely glancing at the hard hats, hammer, and plastic sheeting beneath them. Jason knew he would probably never use any of the other stuff. Sam had a habit of just taking what he could, regardless of the item's usefulness to him later. And Jason had a habit of doing what Sam told him to do. The 'ole sleeping pills in the tea that night had also been Sam's idea.

Sam wasn't all bad news and bossing Jason around, though. He was tough, a good friend to have on your side when things went south. It also didn't hurt that he worked at the local animal shelter, had the keys, and knew exactly where that days' euthanized pets were stored.

Every Wednesday, Sam had to stay late with one of the

local veterinarians while they euthanized all the cats and dogs no one wanted to adopt. Well, that wasn't entirely true. The shelter held the super-cute ones for a little longer than a week, along with the puppies and kittens. But never the old or aggressive ones. Those almost immediately went to the back row of kennels after intake, what the workers all called "The Farm". Because that's what every parent tells their kids. "Spot just went to live on a farm for old dogs, he's very happy there." Said with a straight, sad face, even as Old Spot's corpse stiffened in a plastic grocery bag in the freezer. Behind the peas, of course. You couldn't run the risk of little Susie finding it before trash day.

The animals on "The Farm" at the shelter were destined for that same fate, they just usually skipped the bit about hiding out in the freezer first.

Jason lifted the garage door halfway, patting himself mentally on the back that he had thought to spray WD-40 on the squeaky bits a few days before. He was tall and had to crouch low to fit beneath the metal door. He eased it down behind him. As big and as loud as it could be, it still seemed smarter than leaving through their front door. Gretchen had just purchased one of those doorbell cameras that alerted her phone when anything moved on the front porch.

He slipped his flip-flops on and walked to his car parked a few houses down. He moved it earlier when his dad took a shower and Gretchen watched TV in the living room, sipping on her fourth gin and soda.

It was a short ride to the shelter, and not a cop in sight.

Jason eased onto the shoulder half a block away, turned off his car, and waited for the vet to leave. He ducked down in his seat and pulled out his phone, holding the screen low so it couldn't be seen from the road. The heat from the day still hung in the air, and he wished he could roll a window down.

Cat Food

At least they were doing this at night when it was slightly cooler. Jason wiped small beads of sweat from his forehead then took his baseball cap off, smoothed his short blonde hair back, and put the hat back on. As he shifted in the seat, his legs separated from the leather, breaking the damp suction with a smack. He should have rolled down a window or something but didn't want to risk being seen. But it wasn't long before he looked up in time to see the vet open the front door. Her lab coat fluttered behind her as she beelined it to her car. He slid down further as her pickup truck drove by, though he knew he didn't really have to worry about her. She focused on only one thing that night; getting home, pouring herself an entire bottle of Cabernet, and watching reruns of *Friends*. She hated Wednesdays at the shelter and always ended it with that same routine. Jason knew this, because back when the vet had first started, she had been talkative with Sam, even friendly. But then it slowed until she barely spoke at all as she injected Sodium Pentobarbital into the hearts of all those abandoned pets.

Once she took a right on Oak Drive, Jason turned the key in the ignition and drove toward the animal shelter. He parked next to Sam's yellow Mustang in the front parking lot and got out, slamming his door behind him.

"Hey!"

Jason looked up. Sam ran through the front doors, waving his arms and straining to get his attention without making too much noise. His compact legs were pumping. Jason was much shorter than him and stocky. He worked out every chance he could get and it showed. His shirts were always tight against his arms, but he still had trouble getting the ladies' attention. No matter how strong you were, some chicks just didn't dig a short dude. Didn't stop him from trying, though.

"No, dumbass! Park in the back! Jesus."

"That's what she said," Jason laughed.

"I'm serious, would you fuckin' go?" Sam huffed.

"The fuck was I 'sposed to know?" Jason shook his head, climbed into his car once again, and drove behind the building.

He parked and stepped out, careful not to slam his door. The thud of it closing behind him echoed in the silence. It was eerily quiet, with no animals barking, no street traffic, and no one else there besides the two of them. Jason had never been to the shelter at night and the way the woods behind the building faded into pitch black made him uncomfortable. He rushed to the back door. In and out. Sam had said they'd be in and out in less than twenty minutes.

A red chipped brick held the door open and a shaft of light spilled out into the night. Jason shoved the brick out of the way with his foot and walked through the door, coughing. No matter how many times he visited, he would never get used to that scent. Urine, feces, and body odors from a hundred animals. Then there was the underlying aroma of bleach that, in his opinion, they could always use a little more of.

The stillness outside continued within as if an infection had seeped into the building. Normally you couldn't even wiggle a doorknob without setting off howls from every cage, but on Wednesday nights it's like they knew what had happened to their former cellmates and thought it best to lay low. They were awake, however, and aware. As he passed the open door to the kennel room, all eyes locked on Jason. Some brown, some hazel, some bright blue, and some so dark they made the hair on his arms stand up. All of them tracked his movements, not missing a beat.

During his other visits, always after hours so Sam could let him in the back door, Jason felt like a walking sausage...as

Cat Food

if they were just waiting for their chance to devour him. But that night they didn't seem hungry or aggressive, just watchful.

"Sam?" Jason whispered into the darkness. Up ahead, a faint glow shone beneath one of the doors.

"Back here!" Sam answered from behind the door.

Jason pushed the door open and gasped.

"Shut the door, don't wanna freak out the others any more than they already are," Sam said as he shoved dead dogs and cats into black plastic bags. "These here are mine, those over there are yours."

Jason's eyes widened as he took in the pile of fur on the floor. The cold room smelled of bleach and french fries. His eyes watered from the strong cleaner. Confused, he looked around until he noticed the takeout paper sack next to Sam.

"Well, don't just stand there, grab one and start stuffing!" Sam said as he stopped to grab a handful of fries.

Jason stared at him.

"What? I got it for lunch but didn't get a chance to finish before that bitch made me go back to work." He shoved the fries in his mouth.

Jason scrunched up his nose and shook his head, then turned back to the bodies on the floor. "I brought the bags you told me to…"

"I found these in the back," Sam interrupted.

"Ok." Jason pulled a bag from the roll on the table, opened it, and shook it out. He looked at the dead animal closest to him. It was a black cat, just like Raven, the one he used to have before they got Bertha. Raven had been killed by a dog on the sidewalk in front of their house. Jason had been the one to find her on his way home from school that day. She was stiff by then, and he never forgot those cold, dead eyes. He looked down at the cat, still holding the plastic in his hands and not moving. Jason knew it wasn't Raven, couldn't have been. But the resemblance....

"Dude, we don't have all night!" Sam grunted as he tried to pull the wide plastic strings at the top of another bag. A dog's leg stuck out, preventing it from closing. Sam shoved it back down and tied a knot with the strings. "What a pain in the ass." He wiped the sweat off his forehead with the sleeve of his shirt and reached for the next one.

By the night's end, Jason had packed up five dogs and eight cats, and Sam had packed six dogs and ten cats.

"I'm not sure this adds up," Jason said as he looked at Sam's stack, then back again at his own.

"I did most of the work and it's my ass on the line, anyway. I think it's more than fair," Sam grunted as he hefted one of Jason's bags onto a cart.

One by one, they loaded Jason's haul into the trunk of his car. The night remained still, only the crunching of their feet on the gravel and the thunk of the animals landing in the trunk breaking the silence.

Sam stopped and leaned against the back of the building. He pulled a roach from his pocket, straightened the bent ends, and lit it.

Jason glared at him. There were still three bags sitting on the ground in front of his trunk. "Really? You think *now* is a good time for that?"

"What? I helped with the others. Want me to do everything?"

Jason closed the trunk and pulled his keys from his pocket.

"Where do you think you're going?"

He reached for the door handle and rested his hand on it. "Home"

Sam tossed his own keys to Jason.

"Pull my car around so we can load mine up. I wanna

finish this. That bitch won't let me take smoke breaks anymore."

Jason sighed and replied, "Sure, why not? Did she *ever* let you smoke that?"

Sam smiled. "She never asked, I never said."

When he returned, Sam had gone back into the building and the door had once again been propped open with the brick.

Jason backed the car up next to his own, pulled the keys from the ignition, and stepped out of the car.

"Sam?" His voice echoed through the darkness ahead. Something rustled in the trees behind him, and he went through the door and closed it without looking back. Jason intended to creep again past the doorway to the kennel room. He couldn't handle all that...*quiet*, and those eyes. But he stopped and peeked around the corner when a high-pitched whimper echoed from the room. There, in the middle of the floor in the most adorable pile of brown fluff, sat a small puppy. Large dark eyes stared at Jason as he tip-toed across the room. A black Labrador shifted in a cage to his right, eyeing him but remaining quiet. On his left, a white pit bull mix chased something in his sleep, with small whimpers and his legs twitching as he ran into the unknown.

Jason reached the puppy and bent down to pick her up. She was heavier than he thought she'd be. Just solid puppy fatness. She settled into the crook of his arm with a sigh. Her fur was fluffy and brown with black streaks throughout. For a moment, he contemplated tucking her inside his jacket and taking her home.

"Dude, what're you doing?" Sam called from the doorway. "Put it back and help me finish this, I gotta meet Rudy in a few to get some more grass."

"Where am I supposed to put her?" Jason looked around as he scratched behind the puppy's ears.

Sam pointed to an empty cage, the door still closed and locked tight. "Shove it back in there. It must have crawled through the bars."

Jason opened the metal door and placed the puppy onto a tattered red blanket. He closed and locked the door and stood up.

"How you gonna keep her from gettin' out again?"

"I don't give a fuck, now come on," Sam said as he walked to the rear of the building.

Jason looked around the room, spotted a wooden board in the corner, and placed it in front of the bars of the cage, covering the bottom half.

"There, now you're kind of safe," he whispered.

She waddled toward the bars and looked up at him, whimpering. He locked eyes with her before sighing and standing back up. Jason walked back outside, where Sam had already loaded two of the pets into his trunk.

"'Bout damn time, you done fuckin' around?" he grunted as he picked up a bag.

"I went in looking for you, ass-wipe."

"I had to take a shit." Sam looked at him before reaching for another. "That all right with you?"

Jason rolled his eyes and helped him load the rest of the animals in silence.

2

Jason backed his car into the driveway and turned the ignition off. He sat in the darkness, his stomach rumbling with hunger. Their dinner that night had been sparse, as usual. A few veggies from his dad's garden in the backyard, sautéed in a little bit of water to keep them from sticking to the pan. Oil was expensive so they tried to ration what little they had, saving it for the company that never came over and special occasions that never happened.

Jason hoped the sleeping pills were still doing the trick, and briefly considered a world where they never woke up. He would have finally gotten revenge for his mother's "accident." The state couldn't prove it in court, but Jason and his older sister, Carrie, were pretty sure their dad had been responsible for their mother's death.

Carrie was twenty years older than him and had been the mom in his life ever since his own died. Jason's conception had been the unsuccessful "save our marriage by having a child" child. The divorce had finalized three days after he turned two years old, and their dad claimed he met Gretchen a few

Cat Food

months later when he skipped an AA meeting to go to a strip club. She had headlined that night, and her golden tassels mesmerized their dad to the point of him proposing that very night in the parking lot when she got off work. That had been their official love story, anyway. Carrie had never believed that bit and liked to tell Jason that their bond was probably sealed in a private VIP room in the back of the club while he and their mom were still married. An extremely bitter custody dispute followed. Carrie and Jason had taken their mom's side, of course, which only served to motivate their dad more to get custody of them. His dad was a classic narcissist; not wanting them because he cared, but because he wanted to *win*. He ended up with custody by default when their mom had been killed.

Their mom had taken their dog, Nico out for their usual walk. She would take him out every evening after they ate dinner, like clockwork. Nico was an extremely high-energy dog and if he didn't get his walk in, he would become unbearable in the evenings, bringing his toys to everyone and whining until they played with him. Their mom had been in the middle of crossing the street at the corner of Wilkins and Polk when a car (or a van, or a truck... they never found out who did it) plowed into her and Nico. The cops said she probably didn't feel anything. Both had died instantly. Nice and tidy. Convenient.

Their dad had acted shocked and sad at the news, even crying a few fake tears in front of the cops. Carrie and Jason's tears were real.

He eased the garage door back open and pulled a string to a light hanging from the ceiling. The bulb clicked on, illuminating one side of the garage. His stomach grumbled again, and a sharp pain caused him to wince, surprising him. It had been a while since he felt hungry. He did all the time toward

Cat Food

the beginning but then, like everyone else, he became used to it and noticed it less and less. Hungry was just what they all *were*. It wasn't only his family, it was everyone. Carrie and her husband, Sam and his family, and all their friends and neighbors. The whole country was hungry. Jason rubbed his stomach, took a deep breath, and opened the trunk of his car.

Thanking Sam for being able to get them the stuff while it was still fresh, he pulled each of the bags from his car and laid them next to the deep freeze against the far wall of the garage. Once full of his dad's deer and hog meat, the freezer had sat empty for years. The day before, Jason had grabbed it by the edge and shifted it away from the wall with a grunt. He blew away the dust, found the old cord, and said a quick prayer to any god who would listen as he plugged it back in.

Jason held his breath while opening the top of the freezer. A blast of stale, cold air hit him in the face, and he smiled. The old girl still worked. He jogged to the car and closed his trunk. He glanced up and down the street, but he needn't have worried. No one was out on that hot summer night. No one was out much anymore at all. The less you moved around, the fewer calories you burned, and they were all thin enough. He eased the garage door down with a soft thud and walked to the pile of bags. As he dropped each animal down into the freezer, he thought of that puppy again and what each of the dead things looked like when they were young. Were they sweet? Did someone love them and take care of them? He shook off the thoughts. He knew it wasn't optimal. It wasn't what anyone *wanted* to do. But it was what had to be done and he knew once he talked to his dad and Gretchen, and Carrie and her husband Manny, that they would agree. He had saved them all; they had to see that.

He closed the top of the freezer and picked up the last bag. It didn't seem as heavy as the others, a perfect specimen to

Cat Food

begin with. Jason opened the door to the house and peeked toward his dad's room down the hall. The door remained closed, and no light showed from beneath it. He breathed a sigh of relief and quickly walked to his room. Beneath a blanket, on the far side of his bed out of sight of the door, sat an ice chest. A plastic sack full of ice from Wick-Mart sat in the bottom. He had prepared it all earlier before his dad got home from work. Jason placed the bagged animal on top of the ice with a crunch, closed the lid, and covered it again with the blanket.

Piece of cake.

He smiled at how smoothly everything had gone as he headed toward the kitchen.

Bertha waited on the other side of his door and jerked back from him as he entered the hallway. She sniffed the air around him, laid her ears flat against her head, and hissed before running into the kitchen. The plastic square of her cat door flapped against its frame before settling to a close.

"Whatever. Be happy it ain't you," Jason said.

In better days, their kitchen had been bright and cheerful. But the sunflower-yellow walls had faded to a murky tan, the table in the middle of the room wobbled no matter how many things you wedged beneath the legs, and the plastic backing on the chairs had all cracked, scratching the shit out of anyone who wore shorts. He opened the fridge and stared at the empty spaces where food used to be. Leftovers had become a thing of the past. A few ears of corn and some squash sat on the middle shelf, and off-brand cokes and Miller Lite were on the bottom shelf. Next to the beer sat an unidentifiable casserole from Mrs. Billie Jean down the street sat on the middle shelf. That would be tomorrow's dinner, he knew, and it looked disgusting. Rumor had it that Billie Jean ate canned cat food, and he had no desire to consume anything that came from her kitchen.

He turned away from the fridge empty-handed and decided to take a shower before he did anything else. Bertha was right, he reeked.

3

Carrie chopped vegetables for soup when she had to stop and look up at the television. At the time, she didn't even know why she tuned in at that exact moment. Perhaps between each crunchy slice of carrot and the thud of the knife against the wooden chopping board, her subconscious had picked up on something different. A change in tone, maybe, or the way someone could ask a question, and even as the other person responded with a "what's that?" their brain had a chance to catch up and they already knew the answer.

"Turn that up," she gestured toward the TV with the knife.

Her husband Manny, sitting on the couch while half-watching the news and half-playing on his phone, reached for the remote. Their baby daughter, Olivia, snoozed in a pink bouncy seat on the floor in front of him. She had her father's dark complexion and her mother's height. Her feet dangled off the end of the seat, one in a frilly green sock and the other bare. The sock lay discarded beneath her.

An exterior shot of the Brazoria County Animal Shelter filled the screen, then the reporters cut to a traffic jam on I-10.

"That son-of-a-bitch did it."

Cat Food

Manny had already returned to his phone. He looked up and asked, "What?"

"Jason. He broke into the animal shelter." Carrie finished chopping and tossed the vegetable scraps into a bag before putting them in the freezer. "What a dumbass."

She dropped the cut carrots into a pot of water on the stove with a splash and turned the dial until it clicked on.

"Are you serious? I thought he was just kidding."

"Yeah, I'm serious. *He* was serious. He's hungry, Manny. What do you expect?"

"I expect him to eat what the rest of us have to eat. What makes him so special anyway? We're *all* hungry." Manny stood up from the couch and stretched. He glanced at the baby before joining Carrie in the kitchen. "Speaking of eating, when's lunch gonna be ready?"

"When it's ready." Carrie glared at him before pulling her phone from her back pocket and pulling up her little brother's number. He answered after the first ring.

"Jason? What the hell did you do? Are you a fucking idiot?"

She paused to listen.

"Okay."

"But-"

"You can't just-"

"Are you gonna let me fuckin' talk?!"

Carrie stared at her phone in disbelief. "The asshole hung up on me!"

"Easy, you're gonna wake Ollie," Manny said gesturing to the sleeping baby. "And I don't know why you're freaking out, it's not our problem."

"His problems *are* our problems, Manny. What do you think Dad and Gretchen are gonna do when they find out?

Whose couch is he gonna have to sleep on?" She jabbed her finger toward their living room. "Ours."

"It wouldn't be the first time." Manny shrugged.

"It's illegal, Manny, and *gross*. And stop calling her Ollie, her name is Olivia."

4

He knew he shouldn't have told that bitch. Of course, she wouldn't think it was a good idea, she'd been shitting on his plans since their mom died and she crowned herself "Supreme Mother." God, she needed to get off his back. Jason didn't even understand why she had her panties all in a wad, it's not like he kidnapped the neighbor's pets or microwaved Bertha. He wasn't a monster, for fucks' sake. He just took what was gonna be trash anyway. The unwanted.

Jason dropped his phone on top of his gray comforter and stared at the ceiling. He followed the fan's slow movement above him until the circles blurred. He wasn't planning on getting up that early but thanks to Carrie, his bladder also screamed at him. He swung his legs over the edge of his bed and cracked his door open. The empty hallway loomed in front of him. His dad yelled at him whenever he wore his boxers around the house, but there was no sign of him or Gretchen. Both had already gone to work. Jason shuffled barefoot down the hall to the bathroom wearing nothing but his red plaid boxers.

He loved those moments when he had the whole place to

himself. He and Sam had talked about moving out and getting a place together, but they hadn't made any actual plans yet.

He left the bathroom and walked toward the kitchen. Usually, his dad left a little coffee in the pot for him, but that morning it had already been rinsed out and laid upside-down on the drying mat.

"Assholes," Jason muttered as he grabbed a coke from the fridge. The least they could do was leave him the rest of the coffee.

He plopped down on the couch, switched on the TV, then remembered his phone still lying on his comforter in his bedroom. Local weather filtered down the hallway from the living room and Jason grabbed his phone and hurried back. The Channel 12 weather chick looked hot, he never minded watching her.

By the time he sat down, they had already returned to the main news anchors. Jason sighed and checked his notifications on his phone, only half listening to the news reports. He was scrolling through Instagram when the words "local animal shelter" blurted from the TV. His head snapped up and he dropped his phone on the couch cushion.

"Oh shit," he whispered.

There it was, clear as day, the shelter he and Sam had just left the night before. Apparently, the staffers noticed the dead animals missing when they got there that morning and reported it to the police.

"Shit, shit, shit..."

Keeping his eyes on the screen, he felt around the couch for his phone and brought it up in front of him. He pulled up the text messages between him and Sam, but there wasn't anything new. Maybe Sam still slept.

Jason called him. "Pick up... Pick up..."

Eyes still on the TV, he tuned out the ringing phone and

listened. They were saying Sam was a "person of interest." He bet anything that bitch vet ratted him out, said he had stayed behind after she left, and that he probably did it. But they also said they were still investigating and couldn't get in touch with Sam. Jason knew what that was like. The ringing stopped as the call went to voicemail.

"Sam, answer the fucking phone! Call me back when you get this."

The news changed to a ribbon-cutting ceremony at some bullshit place no one cared about. Jason thought about going over to Sam's house, but what if the cops were watching it? What if they were over there right then and saw Jason had called Sam's phone? He needed to lay low for a bit, no one had to know he had been a part of it. Carrie was the only one that knew they were considering doing what they did but as much as she liked to bitch at him, she'd never turn him in. He knew Sam didn't blab. He was pretty smart that way. No one said *Jason's* name on the news.

For the moment, he felt safe.

His plan had been to cook the meat from the ice chest in his room and have it ready on the table when his dad and Gretchen got home from work. It would be harder to argue against him with the food right there in front of their faces, presented just like beef, hog, or deer. He wasn't sure what dog or cat tasted like, or which meat it came closest to even *looking* like. He read somewhere that human meat tasted like a combination of beef and pork. They didn't call it "Long Pig" for nothing, he guessed.

He walked back down the hallway where Bertha sat in front of the door to his dad's room, staring at the white wooden door. She turned to watch him walk by, but never budged from her spot.

"Whatever, you're fuckin' weird," Jason said as he continued to his room.

He pulled on a pair of jeans and a t-shirt, then opened the ice chest. The thick plastic made it harder to cut through than he thought, which he supposed was a good thing. No drippage. Jason pulled a pocket knife from his nightstand and cut into the bag. He hadn't noticed the night before whether it was a dog or a cat, and if he was going to have to cut it up, he needed to have an idea of what he had gotten himself into.

The plastic parted to reveal the head of a cat. A formerly white, now something cold and gray, cat. He twisted the piece of cut plastic around until he couldn't see the animal anymore and closed the lid of the ice chest. Jason went back into the hallway, passing Bertha again on his way to the living room. She didn't turn that time but continued staring at the bedroom door in front of her. Jason shook his head and plopped down on the couch.

He grabbed the remote, put a baking show on even though he never baked a day in his life and didn't plan to, and pulled his phone from his pocket. He liked the accents of the contestants and liked watching the stuff they came up with. Maybe one day he'd bake. Either way, it made for good background noise as he searched the internet for how to skin and clean a raccoon. He figured it was the closest to a cat there could be, and no one pulling his search history later would accuse him of eating a cat.

"Hopefully there really is more than one way to skin a cat," Jason chuckled to himself.

The sun lowered in the sky, shining through the big window in the living room as it continued its descent.

He regretted not taking a bigger interest in going hunting with his dad all those years back when they still could do things like that. All that remained then were fishing and crabbing and even though they lived on the coast, the Texas Wildlife and Fisheries Department closely patrolled everything from the bayous to the bays. With so many looking to fish for their meals, the risk of overfishing increased, and then they'd all be fucked. They still allowed you to buy a fishing license but severely restricted the amount you could legally bring home, and his dad always hit his limits too soon. They would greedily eat fish for every meal before it ran out, instead of rationing it like Jason always said they should do. He thought maybe they didn't trust him not to steal it again from the freezer when they weren't looking.

5

Carrie and Manny had worked nights for as long as they could remember. They were both dispatchers for the Clute Police Department, and the Captain had been nice enough to put them on the same schedule. Otherwise, it would have been nearly impossible to spend any time together. If they had to pay for a real babysitter, they would have been on separate shifts as soon as Olivia was born. But luckily, Manny's mom had offered to watch the baby to help them save on costs. Still fuming from the situation with her brother, they dropped Olivia off at her grandmother's and drove to work that night in silence.

"I mean, what was he thinking!" she pounded on the steering wheel with her hand.

"I don't really see what the big fuckin' deal is, Care. We're not the ones eating it," Manny said.

"I know, I just... He's my little brother, Manny! And he could get arrested for this! What would that look like for us?"

"That's what you're worried about? What everyone at work will think of you if your brother is arrested?" Manny turned his head back to the road and shook it in disbelief.

"No." Carrie raised her voice. "Of course, I'm worried about him getting in trouble but don't be naïve, Manny. You know they'll talk."

"No more than they talked when Sgt. Lopez's wife got that DWI. That's the benefit of a small town, you can sweep that shit under the rug. Now, aren't you glad we didn't apply to Houston when they were hiring?"

"Just shut up." Carrie turned the radio up and drove the rest of the way to work in silence.

When they arrived, it seemed business as usual. No one talked about the break-in at the shelter. It wasn't relevant to anyone else but Carrie and Manny. To the rest of the dispatchers, it remained a small line item at the end of the blotter from the day shift. Nothing of interest.

Halfway through their shift, however, all of that changed.

6

The cast iron pan sizzled as it cooked the cat meat, and Jason's stomach wrenched in pain, remembering meals past. Meals he never thought he'd get a chance to eat again. Surely once they smelled it, his dad and Gretchen would be eager to eat and thankful he had helped out. Jason pulled a piece from the pan, placed it on a cutting board, and dug around in the drawer for their old meat thermometer. He wiped the dust from it and popped it into the meat. There wasn't a temperature marker for "cat", so he went with the beef guidelines. Jason always liked his steaks on the rare side and figured cats and dogs couldn't be much different. He pulled the thermometer from the meat and a few drops of blood oozed up from the small hole.

"Perfect," he said, before cutting off a bite-sized piece and popping it into his mouth.

"Ohhhhhh, this is *it*," Jason moaned as the juices ran down the back of his throat, the charred edges rough against his tongue. He would have preferred to cook it in butter, but all dairy products were also off-limits.

He ate the rest of the meat on the cutting board, knowing

he still had plenty to cook for the others. Jason seared the rest of the meat with a full belly, enjoying the scents wafting around the kitchen without the growls and pain from his stomach. He glanced at his watch; it was almost time for his dad and Gretchen to get home. He quickly pulled the rest of the meat from the pan and let it rest on the cutting board before slicing it and placing it on three plates. They still used his mom's dish set, tan plates with brown plants and flowers swirling around the edges. If Gretchen had known they were his mom's plates, she would have broken them all years before. She just assumed his dad had picked them up and joked about his shitty taste in dishes.

Jason set each one down on the table in front of their usual seats. He pulled a fork and knife from a drawer and put one on each side of the plates. He tilted his head and looked at the arrangement before moving them both to the right side. He had no idea what the proper layout looked like, but it seemed pretty good to him. Jason plopped down in his usual spot. They would be home any minute.

He looked at the table and smiled.

7

"271 to Dispatch."

"Come in, 271." Carrie glanced at Manny in the chair next to her and wiggled her eyebrows. There had been a running joke that Officer Barton (271) had a crush on Manny ever since Barton drank too much at the Christmas party and lingered a little too long hugging Manny goodbye.

Manny rolled his eyes and turned back to the display panel in front of his own station. The dispatch room consisted of a semi-circle of monitors, computers, keyboards, and microphones with two rolling chairs inside. Typically, one dispatcher answered the 911 line and the other handled the police, fire, and ems calls. Though that never really mattered, everyone helped out where they could on those rare nights when the shit hit the fan.

"10-38 at the corner of Plantation and Highway 288, northbound. 10-28 on Texas GKA-01Z2. Yellow Ford Mustang."

"10-4," Carrie answered, her brow furrowed. Sam drove a yellow Mustang. She swallowed and sat up straight as she entered the license plate into the database and waited, hoping

Jason wasn't with him. The panel to her left finished searching, showing the results on the small black screen.

"Ugh, it *is* him," Carrie said to Manny before pressing the button. "Dispatch to 271, Plate comes back to a Sam Dorren. 10-69?"

Carrie waited while the officer moved toward his patrol car so Sam couldn't hear the radio. Manny turned to listen.

"Dispatch, go ahead with 10-69."

"Owner possibly involved in a breaking and entering on the 23rd of this month. Wanted for questioning by Lake Jackson PD."

"10-4"

Carrie chewed on her fingernail and waited for Barton to confirm it was Sam driving the Mustang. Manny whispered, "Of course it's him, it's his car. I bet Jason's there, too."

"Shut up," Carrie hissed at her husband before the radio crackled, interrupting them.

"271 to Dispatch, 10-27 on TX 686368382."

"10-4, standby."

Manny read the screen over Carrie's shoulder after she punched in the driver's license number and whistled. "I told you."

Carrie sighed. "Whatever, at least Jason isn't with him."

"Dispatch to 271-" The radio cut off with a squeal.

"Dispatch, subject fleeing on foot eastbound on Plantation, requesting backup," Officer Barton huffed into the radio as he ran.

"10-4. Attention all units, assistance requested at Plantation and 288. Subject Sam Dorren fleeing on foot, eastbound on Plantation, white male, 6'3", approx. 250lbs. Brown hair," Carrie spoke into the microphone before releasing the button. She put her elbows on the desk and laid her head on her hands, closing her eyes and taking a deep breath.

Cat Food

The radio squawked again, and Officer Barton yelled out between breaths as he ran, "Blue jeans, white hoodie!"

Carrie looked up and pressed the button. "10-4"

She knew she didn't need to bother relaying the description any further, as two other units announced that they were en route and had heard the descriptions.

Carrie told Manny to call Jason while she arranged for a tow truck to pick up the Mustang. The officers kept searching, but never caught back up with Sam.

8

Jason watched his phone ring until it went to voicemail. He had no desire to talk to Manny or Carrie. He knew what they were gonna say and had grown tired of hearing it. Carrie had acted like his mom his entire life, and sometimes it just got old. He didn't need a mom or a bossy sister. The phone rang again, still Manny. He ignored it again.

The wooden chair legs screeched against the floor as he pulled back from the table and headed toward the bathroom. As he turned the corner into the hallway, he saw Bertha still sitting near the door to his dad's bedroom.

"Hey, girl. You still mad at me?" Jason knelt and reached for the cat, clicking his tongue. "Come here, girl."

Bertha sauntered toward him, her tail held high, twitching back and forth. As she came closer, he noticed a strange odor in the hallway. He reached out to pet Bertha and looked around for the source of the smell but couldn't see anything.

"Did you bring another mouse in the house, girl?" But it wasn't quite like a dead rodent's stench... "Or did you have an accident outside the litter box?"

She pulled back from him as if indignant and ran toward

Cat Food

the kitchen. Jason jumped up and grabbed her before she could get to the dinner table. He didn't think she'd know the chunks of meat were from another cat but didn't want to risk her snatching any of it off their plates before dinner time.

"You can just wait in here until after we eat," he said as he tossed Bertha into his bedroom and shut the door.

After he used the bathroom, he walked back down the hallway to the kitchen. The smell seemed stronger in the hallway, but he didn't have time to investigate it further. He wanted to see the look on his dad and Gretchen's face when they saw the food, so he hurried back to the table.

The minutes ticked by and he ignored four more phone calls from Manny and three from Carrie. Jason kicked his flip-flops off into the corner and looked at the clock again. They were extremely late. He rolled his eyes and sighed. They probably went to the bar and then to see a movie after work. Sometimes they did that without telling him. When he complained about it, their answer had always been, "Well you're hardly ever home anyway, we didn't think you cared."

He *didn't* care but still liked to know things.

"Fuck it," Jason said as he picked up a knife and fork and cut off a small piece of meat. He chewed on it, rolling it around in his mouth trying to savor the feeling. It had been a while since he'd had anything so delicious. Before he realized it, he had devoured his food and washed it all down with a coke. He crumpled the can and tossed it into the trash as his phone rang again. Sighing, he glanced at the device expecting to see his sister's name but was surprised to see Sam's.

"Shit," he muttered, realizing he had stopped trying to get a hold of Sam earlier. Some friend he was... Jason picked up the phone.

"Hey, I'm in some trouble," Sam said, breathing hard.

"Yeah, I saw, the fuck are we gonna do?" Jason said.

"No...not just the news." Sam coughed. "The cops have my car, man."

"What? What did you do? You okay?" Jason grabbed the plates and tossed them in the fridge. He held the phone between his ear and his shoulder and shoved his flip-flops back on.

"Nah, man. You at your house? I'm here in the back. Didn't wanna knock since your dad's home."

"Dad isn't-" Jason walked to the front door and stopped. He tilted his head, waiting to hear his dad's truck pull into the driveway.

"Dude, come on. I'm kind of in a crisis, here."

"Be right there." Jason shrugged and ran to the back door. He had to jerk on the door handle a few times before it would open. The house settled depending on the seasons and in the summer, the back door stuck. He stepped onto the porch and eased the door closed. If his dad had just pulled in, he didn't want him to know he was outside with a fugitive. He squinted into the darkness.

"Where are you?" Jason whispered.

"Over here and keep it down!" Sam hissed from a corner of the yard.

Jason walked to the corner and finally spotted Sam standing beneath an oak tree by the back fence. Sam still wore his clothes from the day before and he stunk like rotten food.

"Dude, shower much?" Jason waved his hand in front of his face.

Sam looked around him toward the house. "Got any of that meat left?"

"Meat?" Jason's brow furrowed in confusion.

"From yesterday. The dogs and cats, man. The *meat*." Sam said as he covered a cough with his hand. The hand almost glowed in the moonlight, pale and bright. His eyes were wide and his face glossed with sweat.

Jason stared at his friend. Sam shifted his weight from leg to leg and scratched his head. When he pulled his hand away, thick bunches of his hair came with it, leaving a bald patch. Sam didn't seem to notice as he repeated, "Do you? Do you?"

"Yeah, of course. What, I'm gonna eat it all in a day?" he laughed, trying to lighten the mood, but Sam walked around him and headed toward the house.

Jason backed up and put his hand on Sam's chest. "What are you doing? You can't go in there, you're all over the news and Dad'll turn you in. You *know* he will."

"So, we'll take care of 'im." Sam pushed against Jason's hand, his eyes glued to the back door of the house.

"Take care of him? The fuck is wrong with you, man?" He grabbed the front of Sam's shirt to hold him still.

Sam flung his head around, inches from Jason. "I'm just so *hungry*. Come on…share." His rancid breath blew into Jason's face and he dropped his head and gagged. Jason opened his eyes and his dinner tickled the back of his throat as he looked at Sam's shirt. Vomit, dirt, and a dark thick sludgy mixture of the two covered the shirt.

He let go of his friend and jumped back. "What the fuck, man?"

"Forget it, I'll go back to the source. Get more there anyway. Fuck you." Sam said as he jogged toward the trees at the edge of the yard. He didn't look back as he came to the chain-link fence, grabbed the metal bar on the top, and hurled himself over. He landed on the other side and kept running.

"What the actual…" Jason said to himself. He looked down at his hands. They were dirty and smelled awful, the puke and dirt all over Sam's shirt had left remnants on his hands. He walked back into the house and washed them three times in the kitchen sink, just to be on the safe side.

Jason turned from the sink and had to grab the back of a chair to steady himself. The room spun around him, and everything seemed distorted as if he had looked through a thick layer of plastic wrap. He touched his forehead and thought it felt warm but couldn't be sure.

"I don't feel so hot," Jason whispered as everything went dark and he slumped to the floor.

9

Carrie screeched into the driveway of her dad's house, threw the car into park, and jumped out. Manny ran after her toward the front door.

"Jason!" They banged on the wooden door with both fists. "Jason!" Her idiot brother was probably asleep, but his car in the driveway proved his presence at the house.

Carrie fumbled in her pocket for her keys and unlocked the door. A powerful odor punched her in the chest and they both coughed and covered their noses and mouths with the front of their shirts. The front hall seemed quiet, and Bertha was nowhere in sight. The cat always greeted Carrie at the door when she would visit; Carrie did half-raise her, after all.

"Jason?!" Carrie yelled, the sound slightly muffled by her t-shirt.

"Where is everyone?" mumbled Manny.

She turned the corner into the kitchen and gasped, the shirt dropping from her face. Jason lay in a heap on the floor. His head and shoulders leaned against the oven door and his mouth hung open. He looked terrible. She dropped to his side and shook his shoulders. Manny stood over them, peering down.

"Umph," Jason mumbled as he opened his eyes.

Carrie exhaled, happy he could breathe. She screamed into his face as she continued to shake him. "Jason! What happened? Are you okay?"

"What the fuck, man?" Manny said.

Jason managed to pull away from his sister in time before leaning over and throwing up onto the kitchen floor. He sat up and wiped his mouth with his shirt sleeve.

"What, are you sick?" Carrie scooted away from him, bumping into Manny behind her. Manny stumbled backward as Carrie sat on the floor.

"Sorry," she said in Manny's direction, eyes still locked on Jason.

Jason turned to Manny, then Carrie. He looked confused, like he didn't recognize them. "Sam..."

"That asshole is nothin' but trouble, I told you a hundred times-"

"What time is it?" Jason asked, looking around for the clock on the wall in the kitchen.

"Six-thirty in the morning, we just got off our shift," said Carrie.

"What-"

"I just want you to tell me why the fuck you think you can just break into places and now your best friend is getting arrested, do you know what this is going to look like for me when they find out? And they're *gonna* find out, it's just a matter of time-" Carrie screamed.

"Shut up!" Jason shouted, holding his head in his hands, "Shut the fuck up for a fucking minute. My head is killing me and your yelling isn't helping."

He looked up at her and said, "Carrie," as if he were just recognizing her.

"You can worry about being sick later. Right now I'm trying to keep you out of jail. Do you know that asshole ran from the fucking cops?" Carrie stood up and grabbed a paper towel from the roll on the counter. She ran cool water over it, then leaned down and pressed it to Jason's forehead.

"What? When?" Jason looked around the kitchen.

"Earlier this evening, she was actually on the radio when it happened. They're looking for him and eventually you, I'm sure. Was there a surveillance camera at the animal shelter?" Manny said.

"I don't know. I don't think so. Sam said he took care of it."

"At least that dumbass did one thing right." Carrie shook her head and stood, reaching toward Jason. "Can you stand up? What hurts?"

"Yeah." Jason ignored her outstretched hand and lifted himself off the floor. He then dropped into a chair with a thud and put his hands on the table as if to steady himself. "Everything hurts."

"Should we go to Urgent Care?" Manny asked, looking at Carrie.

"No, stop worrying. I'm okay. Just a bug. Probably got it from Sam, he looked fuckin' awful. I'll sleep it off-"

"Wait, what? You saw Sam? When?" Carrie yelled, her voice raising with each word.

"Calm your tits. He just stopped by for a second." Jason glanced at the clock in the kitchen. "A few hours ago, I guess. I don't know where he went."

Carrie huffed and sat down across from her brother. She waited until he looked at her before saying, "This is serious, Jason."

"She's right," Manny agreed.

Cat Food

"I *know* that."

"Do you? Because from where I'm sitting, it looks like just another day for you. You never give a shit about anything," Carrie yelled.

Jason stood up and went to the fridge. "If you're gonna yell at me more, is it okay if I eat while you're doing it? I'm starving."

Carrie stared at Manny, waiting for him to come to her defense. Manny shrugged. "You *are* yelling."

Jason pulled the two plates out and set them on the counter. He put one in the microwave before turning to his sister and brother-in-law.

"Hungry?"

"Always," Carrie smiled. She stared at the other dish still sitting on the counter and her eyes narrowed. She stood up and went toward the food. "What..." she jabbed her finger into the top of the meat, "...is that?"

"Your dinner. Definitely yours now, since you put your grubby hands all over it. Y'all can share." Jason pulled his plate from the microwave, put theirs in, and pressed the buttons.

"Is that..." she scrunched her face up, "...a dog?"

"No fuckin' way I'm eating that," said Manny.

"No...of course not," Jason answered before smiling. "It's a cat."

He smiled that mischievous grin that had gotten him out of most things when they were younger. Carrie could never stay mad at him long. He grabbed three forks from a drawer and tossed them onto the table.

"Ugh, how did I know you were gonna say that..." Carrie rolled her eyes as he sat down at the table.

"Just try it, okay? Isn't that what Mom used to always say? You have to at least try it."

Cat Food

The microwave beeped and Carrie pulled the food out. Steam wafted toward her and she closed her eyes and breathed in. "Ahh man, I miss this." Carrie smiled as she sat down. She picked up the fork and pointed it at her brother. "I'm just gonna pretend it's beef."

Manny pulled the chair out next to her and grabbed the remaining fork. "I guess we're doing this. Let me get in there, too."

They ate in silence, the three of them enjoying a meal they thought they'd never have again. With each bite, Jason ate faster and faster, until he shoveled the food into his mouth, barely chewing before he swallowed.

"Easy. Slow down or you'll get sick," Carrie said.

"I'm just so *hungry*," Jason said as he wiped his finger across the plate to get the last few bits of juice. He popped his finger in his mouth and rolled his eyes. "So. Good."

Carrie and Manny laughed. It felt good to laugh, felt good to feel normal for just a few minutes at least. It seemed like ever since the virus surfaced, it was all anyone could talk about.

They thought it first appeared at a meat market in Brazil, but no one could prove it. It then quickly infiltrated wildlife, showing up in deer and hogs. It wasn't like anything anyone had ever seen before. It was fucking *brutal*. Hunters were finding animal corpses covered with a sticky yellow film like it had oozed from their pores. Beneath the film, craters of skin had sizzled away until all that remained were hooves, antlers, or tusks. Their dad had come upon one in the early stages and watched it happen, but no one believed him until the official reports came out.

Then it was just a matter of time before it consumed the factory farming industry, and nothing was safe. Pigs, chickens, turkeys, cattle, lamb. You name it. If it had flesh, it got infected.

Except for cats, dogs, and aquatic life. For some reason, they were spared. The authorities had made it illegal to consume pets, just in case the virus jumped to them. Fish were farmed to near extinction, then protected to the point that the government would rather their own people starve to death than overfish their precious sharks. Almost every day the local news reported on fights breaking out on the shores. The National Guard came in, then it all really went to shit. Each person could only be allowed one fish, two crabs, and one miscellaneous item (octopus, etc.) per week. Only adults of each species were allowed, and no females since they could be carrying eggs. For most people, it wasn't worth the trouble. But the cost of grains, wheat, and veggies skyrocketed due to demand, and Carrie and Sam's dad had, along with most of the population, planted their own vegetable gardens in their backyards.

Pets were harder to come by, as most people had taken to eating their own despite the laws against it. Some abandoned their cats and dogs at the shelter to avoid the temptation. They couldn't bring themselves to eat their cat, but a shot of Sodium Pentobarbital to the heart was totally fine. Fluffy could die, but not by their own hands. Bertha had been declared off-limits by Gretchen pretty early on. Her reasoning was that it didn't make sense to take the cat's entire life for just one meal for the three of them. One meal wouldn't make much of a difference in the long run, anyway, and as long as they had their garden, they didn't *have* to eat her.

"I'm full. Guess my stomach isn't used to this much at one time. Anyway, we need to go pick up Olivia." Carrie leaned back in her chair and sighed. She smiled at Manny. It was good to see him happy for a minute. Fully satiated, and content that her brother would be fine, a nagging thought pulled at the back of her mind. There was something...

"Hey, you need to clean out Bertha's litter box and check for mice. This place fuckin' reeks," Carrie said.

"Agreed." Manny nodded.

"Oh shit, I forgot she was in my room. I didn't want her jumping on the table when I had the food out earlier. I'll let her out when you leave."

"Okay." Another thread tugged at the back of her subconscious, but she couldn't quite put her finger on it.

Carrie and Manny left after making Jason promise to call them if he started feeling worse. They got in their car and pulled out of the driveway when Carrie slammed on the brakes and hit the steering wheel with the palm of her hand.

"That's what bugged me. Where's Dad and Gretchen, if their cars are still here?" She said to Manny.

Carrie pulled the car back onto the driveway.

Manny shrugged, then pulled out his cell phone and dialed Sam's number. "Yo, Jason. Is your dad and Gretchen sick, too?" He listened to Jason talk before continuing, "No, man. Their cars are here. Yeah... Okay... Talk later."

Manny turned to Carrie, her hands still on the wheel and her foot on the brake. "He said they're probably sick also, gonna check on 'em and call us. Let's go home, I'm tired."

Carrie didn't want to leave, but they were already late picking up the baby. The sun rose in the distance as they headed to her mother-in-law's house.

10

Jason hung up the phone and slid further down in his chair. He really *did* feel like shit. He didn't want to admit it to Carrie and Manny; they would have insisted on taking him to Urgent Care and that seemed just way more trouble than he needed. He probably had a stomach bug. At least he still had an appetite. He had just finished off a second dinner and remained famished, like he hadn't eaten in years.

Jason placed his palms on the table and pushed himself to a standing position, then headed for the hallway. Carrie was right, it did still stink. Remembering Bertha, he went to his room and opened the door. The cat hissed and ran past him toward the kitchen. The cat door flapped back and forth before settling still.

"Sorry, girl. I forgot." He glanced around his room to see if she had torn anything up but there was only a crumpled receipt she had pulled from the top of the trash can. He couldn't remember throwing anything away, but shook his head and turned back to the hall. The smell seemed stronger in front of his dad's room. A sick feeling crept into his gut as he reached for the door handle.

Cat Food

Immediately a stench overpowered him, crawling into his nostrils and dripping down into his stomach. He jumped backward and covered his mouth and nose with both hands. Coughing, he bent over and threw up on the carpet in the hall. He stared at the mess as his stomach growled, and he couldn't remember why he stood outside his dad's room.

Jason was famished. He leaned down toward the vomit on the floor but stopped himself just inches from the mess. Partially digested hunks of meat sat atop a yellowish sludge. Jason jumped back in disgust and confusion. He pulled his eyes away from the carpet with every bit of willpower inside him and looked up into his dad's room.

He saw the bed and remembered.

Jason wiped his mouth on his shirt and walked into the bedroom.

Resting on top of their recently purchased King-sized memory foam mattress, beneath a thin green blanket, lay the bodies of his dad and stepmom, Gretchen.

Jason had only ever seen one dead body in his entire life, and that had been enough. He had been nine years old at the funeral of his grandmother, his mom's mom. The woman had looked exactly as Jason had always known her, albeit much more quiet than usual. Her eyes had been closed, and her skin glowed with warmth (later he learned that had been thanks to the makeup artist). She had looked *normal*.

This wasn't the case that day in his father's bedroom.

His dad had always been a robust, intimidating man. Standing around 6', 6" with wide shoulders and a former football player turned middle-aged man's build, in life he had been someone to be reckoned with, and feared. But in death, his already-light complexion had turned pale, with a wet, greenish tint to it. One of his arms draped across the blanket, and the skin there had turned dark, almost like a bruise, where it rested on the cloth.

The face of the man in front of him was no longer anything to fear. His eyelids sat half-open, and a clear-white substance appeared to have leaked from his mouth and nose.

But the most disgusting, vile part of it all were the small white wriggling things all over his father's corpse. Maggots squirmed in and out of the skin, swimming in the holes they had created.

His stepmom had suffered a similar fate but faced away from Jason toward the wall. He had been spared having to look at the damage death had done to her.

Jason sat on the edge of the bed, shifting the bodies. A fresh wave of stench wafted around the room and the flesh on his dad's face jiggled like a not-quite-fully set pudding. He watched the maggots, mesmerized by their slow dance across the flesh. In, out, up, down, left, right.

As the sun rose in the sky, it threw shafts of light through the windows. The maggots continued their ballet, briefly illuminated by the light as they moved to different sections of his dad's skin. They were beautiful.

11

Carrie stared at the baby monitor as the light flashed red with every whimper from Olivia. She groaned and ignored it, hoping Manny would wake up and get to the baby before she erupted into full-blown cries. But of course, he didn't. Manny was either the world's hardest sleeper, or he pretended so he wouldn't have to get up. Carrie swung her legs onto the floor and stood up, but darkness clouded her vision. She swayed and plopped back down onto the bed. She felt for Manny without looking and swatted the comforter over him.

"Hey. Hey, get up."

Manny moaned, "I don't feel good."

"I don't either, but I think I just blacked out so it's on you." Carrie put her arm across her eyes preemptively to block the light that Manny always turned on when he got up to check on the baby. The bed shifted and a yellow glow shone through a crack between her arm and her face.

Manny grunted and shuffled toward the bedroom door muttering, "You owe me."

"Sure, got it." Carrie kept her eyes covered. Olivia still screamed through the monitor until Manny's voice broke in.

Cat Food

"Hey, peanut. What's this all about, huh? You hungry? Welcome to our world, baby girl." The crib blankets rustled, and Olivia gasped between cries, already exhausted from her ordeal, but she didn't scream again. Manny just had a way with her that Carrie could never understand or replicate. It wasn't fair. She had been the one who had carried the baby for nine months, she's the one who gave birth to her, but Olivia stayed a daddy's girl through and through.

Manny kept cooing to the baby as he changed her diaper, then the monitor went silent as the fridge banged shut and a bottle rattled against the kitchen counter.

Carrie sighed and rolled over, shoving her face into her pillow in an effort to block out the light. "Why..." she mumbled into the cotton. Giving up, she turned over again and put her feet on the floor. She waited a minute for the darkness to return, and after a while without anything happening, she stood up and shuffled to the kitchen.

Manny sat at the table, holding Olivia while feeding her the bottle. The baby's eyes were closed but her mouth still worked the nipple. His face glistened with sweat, and he looked pale.

"You okay, babe? You don't look so hot," Carrie said as she poured a glass of water for herself.

"Have you looked in a mirror lately?" Manny said. Olivia's eyes fluttered open, then closed again as she kept sucking the bottle.

"If I look anything like I feel, then I know it's rough." Carrie grabbed cold medicine from the cabinet and sat down at the table. She popped a few of the pills and handed the box and glass of water to Manny. "Here, your turn. Let me take her."

"Oh sure, now you get her when she's almost back asleep." Manny smiled and handed the baby to Carrie. Olivia's eyes remained closed. He stood and kissed the top of Carrie's head as he poured his own water glass. "Not sharing with you, just in case."

"Clearly we have the same bug, dummy." Carrie rolled her eyes and wiggled the bottle free from Olivia. For a few seconds, her lips stayed pursed, sucking a bottle that wasn't there. She settled back to sleep and Carrie used the sleeve of her own shirt to wipe a milk bubble from Olivia's lips.

"I'm starving, want anything?" Manny asked as he pulled soup from the fridge.

"Hell yeah," answered Carrie. "Let me go put her down and I'll be right back."

When Carrie returned, Manny tilted the last of the soup into his mouth.

"Hey! Save some for me," Carrie said, frowning.

Manny set the empty bowl on the table and looked up at his wife, frowning. "Sorry."

Carrie rummaged through the near-empty pantry and produced a stale bag of mini cookies. Once a week the local food bank gave out whatever they had left, usually expired shit. There used to be rules against stuff like that, but that had all gone down the drain along with everything else.

She ate the cookies, then turned back to the cabinet to see what else they had. Manny did the same in the fridge.

12

Jason closed the door to his dad's room and leaned against the wall in the hallway. He couldn't call 911, they'd know what he did and arrest him. No one would care that he didn't mean to kill them, that he didn't know he had given them so many sleeping pills. The truth was, he had killed his dad and stepmom. He looked at the bedroom door and thought he should probably be feeling something, but hunger remained the only thing he knew.

He ate the rest of the cat meat without bothering to cook it first. He wondered why he ever cooked it to start with. Completely raw, it was the most delicious thing he had ever tasted, until he ate a pack of crackers from the pantry. Then *that* had been the best thing he had ever eaten. He downed the rest of the crackers, two bags of chips, three apples, and four boxes of raw pasta. When he finished, he lay on the floor of the kitchen, enjoying the feel of the cool tile against his cheek. Bile rose in his throat and he rolled to the side and puked, not caring that it covered his shirt and jeans. Jason stood up and went to the garage to get more meat from the freezer.

Everything had been frozen solid, so Jason pulled out the

Cat Food

rest of the plastic bags and set them on the floor of the garage to let them defrost. He returned to the kitchen and went through the rest of the pantry and the drawers in the fridge. Sometimes his stepmom hid food behind the tofu, knowing he wouldn't touch the stuff.

Jason chuckled. The joke was on her. He had already eaten the tofu *and* the banana pie pudding hiding behind it, all six containers of it.

He threw up again before grabbing his keys and going out the front door. He climbed into his car and headed back to the animal shelter.

From halfway down the street, he could see two black-and-white police cars and an ambulance parked in front of the building. Their sirens were off, but the lights on top of the vehicles flashed, reflecting off the building like sparklers. The cops stood around the ambulance, one talking to a radio on his shoulder, one smoking a cigarette, and a third staring into the back of the ambulance. The hunger within almost had him stop, but there still remained enough common sense in Jason to tell him that would be a terrible idea.

He drove on, taking a left on Manor St. before heading south down Wilkins. A blue Chevrolet drove past him, but the windows were tinted so Jason couldn't see the driver. Not many other cars were out, that was one advantage of living in a small town. The nights were nice and quiet. Peaceful.

Ahead, a bright patch of lights from the Wick-Mart gas station and convenience store caught his eye. Jason slowed and pulled into the parking lot. He stared, mesmerized by the seemingly endless rows of canned goods, chips, candy, and other food visible through the large glass windows that covered the front of the building. He smiled, turned the car off, and stepped out onto the pavement.

A woman, probably no older than twenty-one, looked up

from her phone when the bell jingled above the front door. Her black hoodie hung on her at least three sizes too large. A boyfriend's perhaps, or maybe she just liked them baggy. A gust of wind blew in around Jason and the silver ring in her septum bounced as she wrinkled her nose.

Jason looked down at the vomit covering his shirt.

"My bad, bro."

He laughed at the clerk and then headed for the food on the shelf closest to him. It was odd, from the parking lot it had seemed like every shelf brimmed with food, but standing in front of them they were all mostly empty. Jason stared at the empty spaces, then back through the large windows to the parking lot and his car. The glass looked normal enough, nothing weird or distorted about it. He shook his head and reached for potato chips, ripped the bag open, and poured them down his throat.

"Yo, dude. You can't do that!" the clerk said as she put her phone down and stood up.

Ignoring her, Jason reached for the only other bag of chips on the shelf, opened them, and ate the entire thing within seconds. When he lowered the bag from his face, the clerk stood right in front of him.

"Dude. What the fuck, man? You gonna pay for that?" She stared at Jason incredulously.

"I don't have any money," Jason said as he turned his back to the clerk, walked past a few more empty spots on the shelf, and stopped in front of a stack of candy bars. He grabbed a handful and shoved them in his pockets before reaching toward a can of tiny canned sausages. Jason pulled the tab on top and opened them. He held the open container over his mouth and poured. Just as the juice hit his throat, the clerk knocked the can from his hands. Jason watched it tumble to the floor, spilling sausages and juice across the aisle.

Cat Food

"Why..." Jason said as he looked up at the clerk, confused.

He knelt and picked up the sausages from the floor, popping them into his mouth before the clerk could swat those away as well. Jason stood and walked to the next aisle, looking for more food.

"Dude, *gross*," the clerk said as she hurried to catch up with Jason.

He held his stomach as it turned and twisted. Bile rose into his throat and he puked onto the empty shelf in front of him. He wiped his mouth and looked down at his hands. A chunk of sausage perched on the back of his left hand atop a smear of half-digested chips and stomach fluids. He licked the meat from his skin and walked toward the chilled section on the back wall of the store.

Behind him, the clerk also threw up after seeing what Jason had just eaten. He looked over his shoulder at the pool on the floor, mingling with his own. Jason dropped to his knees and scooped the liquid and unidentifiable chunks into his mouth with both hands. The clerk grabbed his shoulder and Jason pushed her away with his elbows, trying not to spill the vomit he had been scooping up.

"Dude," the clerk yelled as she grabbed Jason's arm.

Jason picked up the empty can of sausages from the floor and spun around, swinging it toward the clerk. The pull-tab metal top was still attached and it left a streak of blood across her face as he swung. She touched the wound and stared at Jason without speaking or blinking. She backed up and tripped in the vomit on the floor, hitting her shoulder against the edge of the metal shelf on the way down.

Jason watched her fall and looked down at the can still in his hand. He stood and shuffled to where she lay on the floor, his feet slick against the wet tile. She mumbled, holding her shoulder with one hand and the scratch on her face with the other.

Her eyes met his and she screamed, "Don't hurt me. I won't say nothin'. Just go...*please*."

Jason tilted his head to the side, then looked at the food still on the shelves. He needed to eat in peace, she kept trying to make him stop eating. He turned back to her and brought the can down on her forehead. She yelled out in surprise and pain, and he raised it up and pounded it back down onto her nose. Blood spurted on his shirt and face as he continued hitting her with the can until she stopped making noises.

Jason turned back to the floor and continued eating.

13

Carrie lay next to a man on the kitchen floor in a pool of their own vomit, staring at the open refrigerator. They had emptied the majority of the food hours before. All that remained were a few cans of baby formula. From their position, the fridge light behind the formula glowed, creating soft, bright edges around the can. Carrie stared, wondering why they were still there. She vaguely remembered telling the man they couldn't eat it, but at that moment she didn't have a single reason not to. She stood up, grabbed one of the cans, and shoved her finger under the pull tab, breaking the seal open with a satisfying click.

"Give me that," the man said as he stood and fumbled toward the formula in her hand.

The can slipped out of her hand and crashed to the floor, spilling formula across the white tile. Carrie stared down at the mess, then up at the strange man. Frowning, she turned and reached for the other can still on the shelf in the fridge. He also tried to grab that one, but she moved it out of his way before he could take it from her. He grunted and pushed her

Cat Food

against the kitchen counter, knocking the can from her hand. It clattered onto the floor and rolled away from them.

Carrie grabbed a knife from the block by the stove, pulling it from its slot with a metallic swish. She plunged it into the man's stomach, twisting it as she pushed. He stared up at her, his mouth gaping open in confusion. She pulled the knife out and stuck it into the side of his neck. It slid in like a hot knife in a tub of butter. Carrie always loved butter and put it on everything she could. He tried to scream but only a gurgle came out as he fell. Blood spurted onto the floor creating a thick pinkish sludge where it mixed with the formula and vomit.

She walked to the other end of the kitchen, picked up the can, and opened it. As she drank, a baby cried from the other end of the house. Carrie wiped the drops of formula off her mouth with the back of her hand and stared at the off-white smear across her skin. She headed toward the crying noise, licking her hand as she went.

At the far end of the hallway, a door opened into a room. Light from inside poured into the hallway in a narrow slice, illuminating the tan carpet. Inside the room, a screaming baby lay in a crib. The red-faced baby had rolled against one of the hot pink crib bumpers and gotten stuck. Urine soaked the bottom half of its body and the swollen diaper had expanded past the edges of a yellow onesie. A white letter "O" had been embroidered on the front of the clothing and Carrie wondered what it stood for. Beneath the baby lay a white-and-pink striped sheet, dark and damp. The infant had spit up, and Carrie stared at the yellow froth on the baby's chin. She picked up the baby and leaned forward, sniffing its face. Carrie licked the formula off the baby's mouth, and held it up, staring at the bright blue eyes wet with tears. Carrie's hands, wet with urine, slipped and she lost her grip on the baby. The child tumbled to the floor, knocking its head against the leg of a rocking chair before settling into a quiet heap at Carrie's feet. She stared at the baby, tilted her head as if trying to remember something, then left the room to look for more food.

14

Jason ran through the alley behind Wick-Mart, sniffing the air around him frantically. He tripped on a crack in the concrete and fell into a pile of trash bags next to a dumpster. Blood seeped from a hole in his jeans over his knee but nothing hurt. He remembered blood *should* hurt but didn't know why.

A loud, piercing wail echoed through the alley. The screech ebbed and flowed like the tide. Jason never did like to surf.

Delicious scents seeped into the air from the big metal square in front of him. He couldn't figure out how to get to what lay inside and crawled around it, crying. Blood from his hands left smears across the dumpster as he circled. He couldn't remember why the dumpster had bloody handprints on it. Or why there was also blood on his pants and shirt.

"Hey!"

Jason peeked around the corner of the dumpster. A tall blue man stood in front of the open rear door of the store. He held a gray box out to Jason and told him to get down on his

Cat Food

knees. Jason looked down at the blood on his knee but didn't want to make a mess, so he stood and walked toward the man.

A shot rang out from the gray box and a sharp pain drilled into Jason's right arm.

"Owww," he cried as he jumped back behind the dumpster and held his left hand over the wound. That didn't seem fair.

The man yelled at him again, closer and louder than he had before.

Jason sprinted away from the store, driven by some distant, unconscious urge to get to the animal shelter. Behind him, more shots rang out into the night. He wasn't sure why the gray box kept trying to bite him, but he ran until he couldn't hear the loud noises anymore. A few blocks away, Jason passed a group of teenagers smoking in the parking lot of an abandoned store.

"Yo, what's the rush?" they yelled out to him as he passed.

He heard what they were saying, but the words held no meaning as he continued down the road.

Jason stopped once he arrived in the empty parking lot of the animal shelter and put his hands on his knees as he fought to catch his breath. His head weighed a hundred pounds and lights flashed across his eyes before he fell to the ground, exhausted. Bile rose in the back of his throat, but he swallowed it back down, chewing the larger chunks, and stood. He looked at the street, but the blue man and gray box were no longer behind him. He walked to the back of the building.

A red brick sat near the closed door, and he wondered what it all meant. He turned the handle, but the door didn't budge. A window sat in the middle of the door, narrow and tall just about at eye level. Jason picked up the brick and banged it into the glass. It broke, sending sharp pieces flying into the building, and barking erupted from within. He dropped the brick and reached through the opening, feeling around until he located the door handle and unlocked it. As he withdrew his arm, bits of glass still stuck to the frame cut into his skin. He stared at the blood welling up and the flesh hanging in spots.

Jason opened the door and entered the animal shelter.

15

Carrie sat in the kitchen in a pool of spilled baby formula, leftover vegetable soup, and her own vomit, wondering where she could find more food. She leaned against a man's dead body, picked up his hand, and held it in hers. There had been something there, once. Something good and pure.

The front door jiggled and opened a few inches before the chain latch caught it.

"Carrie! Manny! Open the door!" an older woman screamed.

Carrie pulled herself up and walked into the living room toward the noise.

She stared at the latch, pulled taut between the door and the frame. Peeking through the gap were flashes of gray and red.

"Carrie! Open the latch and let me in!"

She shut the door and touched the chain, unsure how to do what the woman wanted her to do. After a few fumbling tries, she succeeded in removing the latch and the door opened.

Cat Food

The woman rushed into the room, eyes frantic and searching. "Where's Manny? Where's Olivia? Are you guys okay?"

Carrie stared at the other woman's short gray hair and how it contrasted with her bright red shirt collar.

"Carrie?" The woman turned to look at her for the first time. "Oh my god, are you *okay*? What happened?"

Carrie's eyes were glued to the shirt collar, then the brown skin next to it, and how it jiggled as the woman spoke.

The woman grabbed Carrie's shoulders and shook her. "Look at me! Where are Manny and Olivia!?"

Carrie laughed. The woman's throat continued to wiggle and the shirt color jumped up and down with each word.

She dropped Carrie's shoulders in disgust and looked at her hands. Something strange covered them, but Carrie didn't care. The woman wiped her hands on her jeans and walked into the kitchen.

"Noooooooooooooooo," she wailed. Her scream was beautiful, from a deep, dark place. It danced before Carrie in shades of red.

"The baby!" The woman ran from the kitchen to a room at the end of the hallway where she screamed again, the sound muffled by something. "Come on, come on, wake up!"

Carrie frowned. Her hunger returned, banishing the dance of red in her living room. She shuffled through the open door and down her driveway. As she stepped onto the street, a baby cried.

She stopped and turned toward the house. A palpation of memory hung in her head, but she couldn't figure out what it dangled from or how it swayed. Carrie stared at the house with one corner of her mouth turned down when the truck slammed into her.

16

Jason left the door open behind him as he walked down the corridor. Snarls and yips continued to ooze from a room off to his right. He stopped in front of the room and peeked in, curious to see if the noises were coming from someone who had anything to eat.

But there was no food, just rows and rows of metal boxes containing loud, furry things. Sharp teeth and mean eyes bore into him as he stepped into the room. In the corner, a tiny fuzzy ball whimpered.

He went to it and knelt down, reaching out his hand. It stepped forward, sniffed him, and recoiled back into the corner. Frowning, Jason stood and left the room.

He took a few steps into the hall before collapsing in a fit of coughs. He fell to his hands and knees onto the chipped linoleum floor. Blood dripped onto the floor in front of him. He wiped his mouth and when he pulled his hand back, a smear of blood had streaked across his skin. Beneath the blood, a circle of exposed flesh tingled. He wiped his hand on his shirt and stared at it again. Thick, yellow pus seeped from the wound.

His legs also burned, and when he pulled his jeans up past his calves, similar craters of raw flesh cried the same yellow ooze.

Jason rolled onto his back and stared at the ceiling. Swirls of white and gray crashed like waves on the stained tiles above him. Something wet touched his cheek and whimpered. He didn't know what it could be, but it felt soft and good. The thing moved toward his leg, sniffing. His jeans were still pulled up, exposing his calf and the wounds quickly spreading across it. Jason registered a faint tugging as the thing pulled on the exposed, raw flesh. It ripped pieces of his leg and growled while it ate.

Jason smiled as everything went black.

THE END

ABOUT THE AUTHOR

Holly Rae Garcia is the author of *Parachute, The Easton Falls Massacre: Bigfoot's Revenge,* and *Come Join the Murder*. Her short stories have appeared online and in print for various magazines and anthologies. She lives on the Texas Coast with her family and five large dogs, and is an affiliate member of the Horror Writers Association. She enjoys reading, watching *Doctor Who*, and playing Texas Hold 'em.

www.HollyRaeGarcia.com

ALSO BY HOLLY RAE GARCIA

Parachute

The Easton Falls Massacre: Bigfoot's Revenge

Come Join the Murder

ROCK
OF AGES

by Rebecca Rowland

For Eric and Bridget: Rock, stick, and scream.

1

It wasn't that Shelley didn't know that rocks weren't food. She wasn't an idiot. It was her stepmother, Diane, who seemed to be confused.

The first incident happened in 1987, when Shelley was only twelve years old. She'd never known her mother, and her father remained a solitary widower until Diane caught his eye at one of his daughter's elementary school recitals. "Winter Wonderland" was the theme, and nine-year-old Shelley, cast as a cheeky ice skater, turned every pair of her white socks a dingy beige sliding about the gymnasium, practicing for the part. Diane, the school's librarian, attended the opening night performance, and as luck would have it, sat next to Shelley's father in the fifth row. They dated for two years before making their union official in a no-frills ceremony at City Hall.

The following summer, Diane sat in an Adirondack chair in their backyard and swallowed five pieces of pea gravel—two grays, two browns, and a speckled white one—while Shelley ran through the sprinkler with two of her school friends. No one noticed. Her stepmother snatched them from the thick layer of landscaping decoration surrounding the rosebushes next to the driveway, allowed them to jingle about her pocket while she made the girls lunch, and then, when no one was watching, tossed them into her mouth: *pop, pop, pop, pop, pop.* Five little jellybeans, no chewing required.

The next week, she moved on to the white marble chips lining the closest neighbor's front walkway. The next month, another yard's crushed bluestone. Vista redstone. Caramel brown river rock. Black lava pebbles. Orange speckled shale. Over the span of one summer, Diane consumed nearly twenty pounds of stones, the equivalent of a hardware store's landscaping starter kit. A rainbow of digestive nightmares.

Around the same time that she progressed from pebbles to full-fledged rocks, craggy bullets that barely squeezed down her esophagus only to be immediately regurgitated or, unfathomably, shat into the toilet a day or so later, neighbors began to inquire about pieces mysteriously missing from their curbside mosaics. "Have you seen anyone milling about my rhododendrons?" the elderly woman who always wore a thick, ivory cardigan draped over her shoulders no matter the weather asked Shelley.

Shelley shrugged her shoulders. "No?" she offered, more an inquiry than a response.

Meanwhile, her father was facing an enigma of his own. "If this keeps up," he yelled, heaving a black-tipped plunger into the bottom of the toilet for the tenth time that August, "we're going to have to call a plumber. Or maybe the city. Maybe the pipes need to be flushed out."

In the living room, Diane fished fluorescent gravel from the bottom of their aquarium with a teaspoon. "Uh huh," she yelled in agreement before shoving the utensil in her mouth, the tiny pebbles rolling around her tongue like defused Pop Rocks.

Two weeks before Halloween, Diane's abdomen had

distended so severely, she could no longer wear anything but drawstring sweatpants. She insisted there was nothing wrong, though she pushed her dinner about her plate like a small child, cutting the food into smaller and smaller pieces, then mashing the bits together to give the appearance of some having been eaten. As her husband blathered on about his frustrating day at the office, she nervously swallowed gulps of water from her glass, one hand pressed against her diaphragm and her face occasionally cringing in a countenance of severe pain. When Shelley's father finally stopped and asked if she felt all right, Diane simply turned her head to the side and vomited, an acidic spray of yellowish-brown liquid soaking the dining room carpet like a firehose.

All told, the surgeons removed fifteen stones from Diane's small intestine, including the one that had lodged into and ruptured her duodenum, requiring minor reconstruction, a soft food and liquid diet for five days following, and a week of bed rest. Strangely enough, they were Arizona river stones, a type of sedimentary decoration no one in the neighborhood used on their property. Her stepmother was ordered into outpatient therapy, twice a week indefinitely, to which she reluctantly complied. When simply talking didn't satiate her strange hunger, Diane began to swallow small orange pills at breakfast and dinner: two oval stones, down the hatch. *Pop, pop.*

Soon after the doctor medicated Diane to a point just shy of walking zombification, Shelley caught her stepmother in the light of the early setting sun, shuffling home from a covert wandering across a nearby flowerbed. Diane carried a paper plate filled with an assortment of rocks of various colors and shapes: a ravenous dinner guest returning to her seat from the buffet.

2

Shelley woke with a start. She'd been waking in the middle of vivid nightmares recently, her stepmother often featured in a starring role even though she hadn't spoken to the woman, let alone seen her, in months. Shelley glanced at the digital clock on her dresser: it was nearly noon. Her head throbbed, a simmering stovetop of nausea swimming over her midsection. She reached for a half-empty can of ginger ale on the window sill where she had left it the previous morning. The contents were warm and flat, and as she drained the last sip, her stomach began to calm, though the headache sat obstinate.

Five minutes later, Shelley dumped her textbooks onto the rickety kitchen table and slumped into a chair. Cate, who had been working on a paper since sunrise, said nothing but raised an eyebrow in her direction.

Shelley had declared a major in biology at the state university not out of sincere interest in the field but from the sheer panic at not having selected a program focus by the time she entered her junior year. She was good at the lab work—excellent, really: efficient and attentive to detail as was needed—

and selecting a science opened up scholarship opportunities. Rather than burden her father with any further financial obligations, Shelley was determined to scrape together whatever was needed to pay her own way.

The campus of the college nestled snugly along the northern border of Massachusetts, a relatively isolated expanse of small town living with little to offer in excursion beyond winter skiing. Her freshman and sophomore years, Shelley spent in a perpetual stupor, trying almost every drug offered to her in the seediest corners of the dormitory tower before finally falling into a small but regular crowd. Cate, a special education major with bright red hair and a rotation of battered bohemian dresses, was assigned as Shelley's roommate freshman year, and they continued to share a room through their final semesters.

In the summer before junior year, they'd moved into the drafty five-room apartment in a broken-down multifamily on Myrtle Avenue because it was close to campus, but the high crime nature of the neighborhood paradoxically coupled with a monthly rent consistent with a prime commuting location forced them to double up on roommates. Cate's boyfriend Aaron, a communications major, snagged the second bedroom and invited his best friend to move in. Thinny, as he was called by just about everyone, not because of his wiry frame but rather due to some nearly unintelligible graffiti scrawled by him on a dorm hall wall and signed with what onlookers could only decode as a T, an H, and a Y (even though his given name contained none of those letters), was an organizational psychology major. Long before they shared a kitchen, their cabal of four made the long trek down to Major's, the townie bar a half mile away, every other evening. The beer was piss warm but cheap and the ID policy mostly nonexistent, and the quartet continued their patronage long after they each turned twenty-one.

Shelley had spent one hour too long and one drink too many the evening before. The late October sunlight streaming through the unadorned kitchen windows pounded a spike into her temples. "I only have one chapter left to read," she explained to Cate. "I'm right on time to work."

Cate smirked and continued tapping on her word processor.

Shelley craned her neck to look through the nearby doorway into the living room. "Where is everyone?"

Cate sipped something from a tall travel mug. Herbal tea, most likely. Of the four of them, she lived the healthiest, maintaining a vegetarian diet tarnished only by a semi-regular overindulgence in cheap vodka. "Aaron had an early meeting at the student union, and Thinny left a few hours ago to meet that chick he was hangin' all over at Major's last night. She's leading some nature walk or yoga in the park or some hippie shit." She sipped her tea.

As if conjured, the front door rattled and Aaron keyed inside, not bothering to remove his jacket as he walked into the kitchen. Behind him trailed a serious-looking woman with multiple piercings along her eyebrows and nostrils.

"Hey, Cate, Shelley, I want you to meet Jess." Aaron turned sideways and held his arm out in the direction of his guest like a game show host introducing a new Toyota.

Cate paused to swallow another gulp from her mug. "Hi," she said finally, then glanced at Aaron expectantly.

Shelley said nothing but nodded at the stranger.

"Jess is here about the room," Aaron continued. He was talking about the third sleeping area, the small alcove that wasn't a bedroom at all but an oddly-shaped dining room off the back of the kitchen. It was large enough for a good-sized bed and modest amount of hand-me-down furniture typical of a college dorm room, but it had no window or closet, and to save on heat, the four roommates had turned off its baseboards the previous winter and kept its door closed tight. Their landlord, however, had raised their rent by two hundred dollars that summer, and they knew that expanding their household by one would offset the cost. "Come: I'll show you the space," Aaron added quickly, and the visitor followed him to the other corner of the room without comment.

Cate raised her eyebrow again at Shelley, who shrugged in response. Cate leaned closer. "She looks older than us. Do you think she's a student?"

Shelley glanced at the open door to the third bedroom. "I'd guess: how else would Aaron know her?"

"Maybe she works with him?" said Cate. Aaron worked second shift stocking shelves at Market Basket, the local supermarket chain. Although the wages were paltry, Aaron was able to score groceries for cost, plus a little extra every week that "fell off the truck." Their cupboards were stuffed with a brick wall of brand name macaroni and cheese boxes, and as the refrigerator's nonalcoholic contents were often limited to an inexplicably large tub of butter substitute and an equally oversized can of ground coffee, the foursome ate more than their share of Kraft powdered cheese.

"I have a check made out for the amount you advertised," Jess said as she reentered the kitchen, Aaron following behind. "I can move in later this week if that's okay?" She shoved a hand into her jeans pocket and retrieved a small folded paper, then held it out to Aaron.

Aaron unfolded the check and frowned. "This is way more than a month's rent," he said, confused.

"That's for the whole year, up to the end of June," said Jess.

Rock of Ages

"I asked my parents for the whole amount. I wasn't sure what you did about utilities."

"We each pay one of them," Cate said quickly before Aaron could respond. "We siphon cable from the guys upstairs, but Thinny pays the phone. Aaron buys the groceries, and Shelley and I split the electricity." She tapped the side of her mug with one finger. "If you'd like to pick up the gas bill, you're welcome to that. It covers hot water and heat."

Shelley turned her head to hide her expression. The gas bill was nearly as high as their monthly rent payment during the winter months. Even after agreeing to keep the thermostat at sixty-three, they'd had to negotiate a payment plan with the gas company the previous year. Cate kept her face neutral, staring blankly at the stranger.

After a long moment, Jess cleared her throat. "Yeah, that's fine. I'll set up an account with the gas company in the morning. The bill will go right to my parents' accountant."

Aaron coughed to stifle a nervous laugh. "Sorry," he explained. "We're not used to having accountants."

Jess shrugged. "My parents want me to concentrate on my studies. They gave me a credit card to use for essentials or extras when I need it, but I don't go out much."

"What are you majoring in?" Shelley asked, then realized the woman might be a graduate student. Cate was right. In the bright daylight, it was clear Jess was at least three if not four or five years older than them.

But without hesitation, Jess responded, "Anthropology. I'm twenty-five, but I'm only in my second year." She paused but continued to stare at Shelley. "I took a few years to travel, plus I did a year at the Campana School in Britain."

Cate frowned. "What's that? Some sort of finishing school?"

Aaron laughed nervously, but Jess nodded, her face somber. "Yes. One of the best in the world, I've been told."

"Women really go to those?" Shelley blurted then felt her face flush pink. "I mean, it's 1995, not 1895. I didn't think people sent their daughters to finishing schools anymore. I didn't even think they existed."

Jess turned to stare at her. "I was incomplete," she said. Her mouth fixed itself in a straight line, and Cate shifted slightly uncomfortably in her seat.

Outside, the sound of a child screaming pierced the air. A moment later, there was a loud bang and the cacophony of glass shattering nearby. "Don't mind that," said Aaron. "Neighborhood kids. When the weather's nice, they are everywhere on the street. They like to play one of three games: rock, stick, or scream."

Jess looked curiously around the margins of the room and shrugged again. "Don't we all." Her eyes stopped on the wall above the stove. "Someone likes to cook." She jutted her chin toward the massive cast iron frying pan hanging above the burners.

"The only action it gets is the occasional pound of bacon on a Sunday," said Aaron.

"It'll double as a weapon should we ever be invaded," added Cate.

The four were silent for a beat, then the front door opened again, Thinny spilling inside. He sauntered lazily into the living room and to the kitchen, his mouth turned up on one side in a smarmy grin. "Hey..." he offered, the word stretching over multiple syllable beats. He wiggled his eyebrows at the group. Despite the relatively cool temperature and full sunlight steaming through the window panes, Thinny was sweating profusely and his pupils were wide and black.

Cate rolled her eyes. "You've got to be kidding me. You are on shift tonight for dinner."

Thinny worked at the campus dining hall. Like Aaron, his take-home pay was minimal, but he managed to snag pizza for the foursome every weekend as well as the occasional warehouse-sized can of coffee. "I clear tables and load a dishwasher all night. It's not rocket science," he said. "Besides, she gave me a parting gift to boot." He reached into his back pocket and pulled out an oversized Ziplock bag folded into a neat rectangle. Inside was a tightly-packed block of grayish-brown. "Where's the jar with the silica gel packets?"

"Above the cereal," said Aaron.

Thinny opened a nearby cabinet, pulled a large canning jar from the top shelf, unscrewed the top, and dumped the bag of mushrooms inside. Before closing the cabinet again, he paused and stared for a moment at the boxes on the lower shelf. "Count Chocula," he said finally to no one in particular. "Right on." He closed the door and wandered out of the room without another word.

"I didn't know we had Count Chocula," Shelley said.

"We don't," Aaron said dryly.

Cate looked at Jess, who was staring blankly at the closed cabinet door. "I'll have a key made for you this afternoon," she said.

3

The fall semester flew by. The five went their separate ways for Thanksgiving but regrouped for the December holidays, celebrating in the apartment Hanukkah with Jess and Shelley, Christmas with Aaron and Thinny, and the Solstice with Cate. These were the only times the original four saw much of their new roommate. Most weekends, she was holed up alone in her room, even when the foursome threw raucous parties or watched movies much too loudly in the living room. She rose and showered early and retired to bed after dinner, and she rarely ventured out at night except for school activities. Odder still was her refusal to let the other roommates into her room. When she left for classes, she locked the deadbolt she'd installed on her door. No one, not even Aaron, who she seemed to like best, had seen the inside of the back room after the Saturday she moved in.

Jess kept her word on the gas bill, however, and when the four stumbled home at sunrise on New Year's Day, they were met with a wall of heat in the normally drafty apartment. "Jesus Christ," Cate slurred, trying her damndest to unwind the wool scarf she'd wrapped around her head as they walked drunkenly home. "It's like a fucking *saunter* in here. I'm going to throw up." She collapsed forward onto the living room couch, one boot still clinging to her stocking foot.

"It's *sauna*, and let's face it: you were going to throw up anyway," Aaron said, sighing. When Cate began to cry softly, though, he rushed into the nearby room he shared with Thinny.

Shelley rolled her eyes. "At least you're predictable, Cate: collapse, cry, puke."

Aaron returned with an oval metal trash can. He placed it on the carpet adjacent to his girlfriend's head.

"Is that My Little Pony?" Thinny asked inquisitively. The three took a step closer to look more closely at the bin. Sure enough, a pastel cartoon of the children's toy dominated most of one side. "Why do we have a My Little Pony trash can in our room?"

Aaron sighed again. "Cate puked in the other one, and I forgot about it and left it over the weekend."

"I thought she threw up in an empty popcorn tin," said Shelley.

"That was Halloween," said Thinny.

Aaron shrugged. "Anyhow, I made her replace it, and this is what she brought home." With that, Cate leaned forward from her space on the couch and vomited squarely into the bin, the wet splash sounds echoing against the metal lining.

Shelley put her hands on her hips. "I'm not surprised. That you forgot about it, I mean. No offense, but your room smells like something died in there. I used to smell it in your dorm room, too. I don't know how either of you have gotten laid in college."

Cate propped herself up and wiped her mouth. "Sorry about this, guys," she said.

Shelley turned and walked toward the bathroom. "I'm brushing my teeth and heading for bed."

"I'm bunking in your bed, Cate," said Thinny. He turned to Aaron. "Good luck with that."

As she lay in her bed, listening to Aaron murmur to Cate in the next room while Thinny's snores reverberated against the walls of hers, Shelley willed her eyes to adjust to the dimness of the room. She knew she should be tired, but she wasn't, and a small part of her grew anxious at imagining the yawning day ahead. Unlike other holidays, New Year's Day seemed more funereal than celebratory: the frigid, muted gray air typical of January in New England; the immense exhaustion folded gently into pillowy hangovers; the stalwart pressure to begin one's life anew with the change in calendar.

In her last two years of high school, Shelley worked as a server and bar back for a local banquet hall. Her father had secured her the position because the owner and quite a few of the kitchen staff were staples in his weekly poker games. The only female employee under the age of thirty, Shelley collected her share of raised eyebrows and wolf stares when she first donned the uniform, despite the Puritanical plain black trousers and white tuxedo blouse. Even after eighteen months of working weekends and holidays, weddings and bar mitzvahs, Shelley hadn't made a single friend at the hall, and she spent her breaks eating her meals alone at the small table reserved for employees in the kitchen or smoking in the overflow bar that was only opened for exceptionally large parties.

In spite of this isolation, she was secretly relieved to be committed to working the days typically reserved for her own family's gatherings. When her boss told her they were overstaffed and would not need her for her second New Year's Day, then, Shelley felt slightly panicked. Shelley's father always spent New Year's Day with Diane, and that year, Shelley had no excuse but to tag along.

As she did for most of the visits at the institution, Shelley sat quietly, her hands folded neatly in her lap, while her father pointed the rickety remote into the air, furiously slamming his index finger into its plastic buttons. The television hovered near the ceiling on a black metal rack like a giant bat. Since Shelley had to crane her neck backwards in order to watch whatever image was flashing about the screen, she chose instead to face her stepmother. Although she was not bedridden, Diane lay on the narrow mattress, a pile of stiff pillows propping her into a slightly upright position.

She pulled on the top of her worn comforter and smiled sweetly at Shelley. "I'm so glad you came," Diane said. She jutted her head toward Shelley's father. "Your dad says you got into a couple of schools already."

Shelley unfolded, then refolded her hands. "Yeah," she replied, "I'm still not sure which one I'll go to. Probably whoever gives me the best financial aid package." She shrugged. "I applied as an undecided major, but I'm thinking I may switch to a lab science once I'm in. I guess I'll see what the classes are like."

Diane sighed but continued to smile. "It's sad," she said. "When your dad and I were in school, you went to college to study what grooved you, you know? You went to school to be educated: you followed your interests and the job opportunities kind of blossomed from there. Nowadays, it seems like people go to college for career training, not to..." Her voice trailed off and she turned her head slightly away as if looking for the end of her sentence that had fallen onto the floor.

"Learn?" Shelley finished, a look of what she hoped appeared convincingly engaged plastered onto her face.

Diane hesitated, then turned to face Shelley again. "Yes,

learn." She sighed again but her face was still cheerful. "I'm so sorry. These pills they have me on...sometimes, they make things a little fuzzy."

Her father stood up and walked progressively closer to the suspended set, continuing to finger-pummel the remote control. Finally, he let his arm drop to his side. "Must need new batteries," he said. "I'm going to ask at the desk if they have any. I'll be right back." Without waiting for either woman to respond, he exited curtly from the room.

Immediately, Shelley felt her back stiffen. Since her stepmother's commitment to the psychiatric hospital four years earlier, Shelley had not been alone with Diane. That arrangement hadn't been orchestrated purposely, but Shelley was grateful for it all the same. What did you say to mentally ill people? Moreover, although she knew it wasn't a rational belief, Shelley's real fear was that Diane would somehow pass along her insanity to her like a transient stranger coughing tuberculosis wetly into the air. She could feel herself holding her breath when her stepmother was near, willing her body to absorb the smallest amount of crazy possible.

When her father sat Shelley down at the kitchen table one morning in the summer before her freshman year of high school to tell her that Diane was going away for "just a short while, just to get the rest she needs, then she's coming home," Shelley knew. Once you were placed in a facility against your will, once you'd been determined to be incapable of rational thought, it was all over. There was no coming home. Not really.

The two sat in awkward silence for a long minute. Then, as if reading her mind, Diane spoke. "I wasn't eating the rocks because I was hungry, you know." She said this so softly, so bizarrely matter-of-factly, Shelley had to consciously focus on the feeling of her feet in her sneakers, the soles pressing against the industrial beige carpet, to remind herself that the conversation was really happening.

Shelley looked down at her hands, the woven basket of fingers she'd assembled. "Yeah, I—"

Diane continued as if Shelley had said nothing. "I know now: sometimes, when we have a hole to fill, an emptiness inside, our primal instinct is to plug it up." She stared straight ahead, at an unseen focal point on the opposite wall. "Some people do it with alcohol. Or sex. Or food. But I ask you—" She turned to face her stepdaughter again, and the saccharine grin reappeared on her face. "Imagine a hole in your backyard. What's gonna fill up that hole faster? A bucket of tequila? A case of Little Debbie snack cakes? A big, smelly cock?" She comically thrust her pelvis up and down, making the bedding ripple. "Or an armful of stones?" She stopped jerking her torso and laughed after she said this: not a short, nervous chuckle but a hearty, uncontrollable guffaw. It was so loud, Shelley felt the tremor of it box her eardrums.

"Diane, I—" Shelley stood up. She would use the excuse that she needed to use the bathroom. Or wanted to change the channel on the television manually. Anything to have a reason to be out of the immediate range of her stepmother. As she rose, however, Diane's hand shot out from under the covers and grabbed Shelley's upper arm.

Diane stopped laughing and her face wiped itself clean of expression. "My point is," she said, her voice returning to its low, even volume, "sometimes, what we ingest isn't always about what we're hungry for. Sometimes, it has nothing to do with hunger at all." She leaned forward, and with her free hand, she peeled back the corner of the bottom pillow to reveal a rainbow of tiny sea glass pieces arranged in a single layer along the cotton sheet, their edges worn smooth and lusterless.

Shelley nodded slowly. She didn't understand what Diane was saying, but she held her breath tightly within her lungs and willed her nostrils to shut. Even after Diane let go of her arm, even after her father returned, tossing a small double-A battery into the air nonchalantly like a coin, and she escaped to the tiny bathroom and shut the door securely behind her, even then, Shelley waited a half second before exhaling. Then she scooped handfuls of tap water into her mouth and spit it furiously into the sink.

In the relative stillness of the overly warm apartment bedroom, Shelley sat up and rubbed her eyes. She resolved to take a short nap in the afternoon. In the meantime, she would catch up on the calculations she needed to finish for her senior thesis: the second half of her independent study was due to begin in three weeks, and although the math had stumped her initially, she thought she might be able to get ahead of schedule and pass in her research early.

She could still hear Thinny's snores behind the barrier of the closed door, but no sound was heard from Aaron and Cate. The living room still smelled faintly of vomit even though Aaron mercifully had taken the soiled trash can into the bedroom with them. Shelley padded softly into the kitchen and opened the refrigerator to grab the can of coffee.

As she did so, Jess's door creaked open, and Jess stood frozen, visually surprised by Shelley's presence. "Oh, hey," she said nervously.

Shelley nodded at her. "Hey yourself. Happy New Year." She glanced down at Jess's hands. Her roommate was holding a gallon of milk. Shelley jutted her chin toward the container. "What were you doing with the milk?" she asked.

Jess shook her head slightly, her dark hair bobbing along with it. "Oh," she shrugged, walking over to the refrigerator and placing the jug inside, "I was just eating some breakfast.

Didn't want to wake you guys by turning on the light." She brushed her hair back with one hand and turned to walk back into her room.

Shelley grabbed the can and placed it next to the coffeemaker. "Ah, cool," she said. "I'm making coffee. You want some?"

"No, thanks," Jess replied quickly. She shut the door behind her without saying another word. A moment later, Shelley heard the deadbolt click into place.

4

They didn't think anything of it when they saw her bring the first few bags home.

"I thought you were getting snacks and stuff," said Shelley, doing her best to unscrew the top from a forgotten bottle of raspberry schnapps. It was welded on tight, the sticky syrup of its contents super-gluing the threads like cement. She rose from the kitchen table and brought the bottle to the sink.

"I'm not on the schedule until Monday," said Aaron, taking a sip of coffee. As he returned the mug to the table, the front door opened and Jess walked in, kicking off her boots and walking straight toward the kitchen lugging a cluster of grocery bags, their secret contents crammed tightly against slippery plastic. She nodded at her two roommates, then rested the bags on the floor in front of her bedroom door as she fumbled with her keys.

Shelley ran the hot water from the faucet and held the top of the bottle beneath the spray. "You wouldn't have chips or crackers or anything in there, by any chance?" Shelley asked, jutting her chin toward the parcels.

Jess picked up the bags and shouldered the door open a

narrow crack. "Hold on," she said, and disappeared with the bags inside. A moment later, she emerged with a gallon of milk and a box of kids' sugared cereal, the kind with pastel marshmallows. "How's this?"

Aaron took the box from her and thought a moment. "Yeah, this should work. Pour it in a big bowl, let people grab handfuls. Kinda thematic, yeah?"

Shelley turned off the faucet and tried the top of the bottle again. To her relief, it finally moved. She emptied its contents into the top of a comically enormous beverage dispenser. Although Jess hadn't inquired, Shelley explained. "We're making psychedelic punch, which is just our euphemism for a mystery concoction of every old bottle of liquor in the house mixed with water and a container of powdered drink mix." She shook the last droplets from the schnapps bottle and motioned to Aaron. He picked up another bottle of liquor from the table and exchanged it for her empty one.

Jess shook off her heavy coat and placed the gallon of milk in the refrigerator. "That's a big container," she said, eyeing Shelley's project.

"Yeah," said Shelley, reaching down and running her finger lightly over the spigot. "Thinny swiped it from the dining hall. They use them for special events. It holds four gallons of liquid. It's just cheap plastic and they throw them out afterward, he said, so one going missing won't make a difference."

"He's our dining hall connection," explained Aaron. "Every now and then, he snags a giant tub of ice cream."

"Or a really unsettling amount of psychedelic mushrooms," Shelley added. "Not from the dining hall, though." She paused, pretending to ponder the idea. "Unless the meal plans have gotten way more interesting since I was a sophomore."

"So," said Jess slowly. "Thinny contributes food, Aaron contributes food. What do you contribute?" She looked squarely at Shelley.

"My delightful personality," Shelley replied without hesitation. She unscrewed another bottle, then looked at its label. "When did we buy banana rum?"

Aaron stood up and stretched. "Shelley is in charge of coming up with drinking games. Don't ever play a game of Operation against a woman majoring in dissection. You'll be on your ass in an hour."

Shelley ran the faucet again and held a glass pitcher beneath it. "We're having a party tonight to kick off the semester." She shut off the sink and poured the water into the punch dispenser, then grasped the tub with both hands and gently shook it, sloshing the contents around. "But this does double duty to get rid of the ridiculous amount of half-empty liquor bottles in the cabinets."

Jess smiled wanly and turned to disappear into her room. "Okay, well, if you're going to hit the supermarket for supplies, I suggest you do it today, and stock up for the next month."

Aaron frowned. "Why? What makes you say that?"

Jess turned back and folded her coat neatly over one arm. "You guys haven't watched the news today?"

Aaron rubbed his hands over his eyes. "I just got up an hour ago. The past two days, Cate's been having these wicked nightmares. Night terrors, more like. She keeps waking up, kicking her legs and screaming for me to get away from her." He patted his shirt pocket to feel for his cigarettes, then slid one out of the pack. "I spend half the night teetering on the opposite edge of the mattress and the other trying to calm her down and coax her back to sleep." He lit the cigarette and blew a stream of white smoke toward the ground, then leaned forward to try to catch a glimpse at his bedroom door on the other side of the living room. "She should be up and around soon. Thinny went home to visit his parents for a few days, but once he's back, the midnight showing's all yours, Shell."

Shelley carefully poured the contents of a drink mix packet into the dispenser. "No, thank you. I'll make do with Thin's snoring."

Jess sighed audibly. "In any case, they are predicting a serious food shortage. It's all over the national news. There's a fungus—"

"Wait," said Shelley. "We talked about this in my Environmental Bio class: the fungus on the grain, right? I thought that was isolated to a few farms in Kansas."

"No, that's just it," said Jess. "It's not just Kansas. The news said that they've found the strain in Oklahoma, Montana, Texas, and the Dakotas." She shut the door of her room and shoved the key deep into her jeans pocket. "Come on. It has to be on CNN." She walked to the living room and turned on the television.

As she did this, Aaron's bedroom door opened and Cate walked out, her ginger hair slightly disheveled about her face. "Speak of the devil," said Aaron as Cate shuffled into the kitchen and over to the kettle on the stove.

"You're not drinking this lemon vodka, are you?" Shelley asked, holding the open bottle over the mouth of the dispenser.

"Not until after I've had some tea, but thanks," deadpanned Cate. She sank into a chair at the table. "This practicum is killing me. Only two weeks into the semester and I am already stressed out."

"So we hear," said Shelley. "Rumor has it, we might wake up one morning to find you stabbing Aaron in his sleep."

"This is it!" yelled Jess from the next room. "Come here and see this!"

Rock of Ages

The four stood in front of the set, Aaron holding his coffee mug and Shelley still carrying the open bottle of vodka. In the bottom right corner of the screen, a small blue rectangle with the words *Talkback Live* appeared, and host Susan Rook, her short brown hair blown stylishly forward, Pat Benatar-style, walked toward the camera, a rippling sea of audience members shifting restlessly in their seats around her. "Gary, what is the Department of Agriculture saying about this sudden and devastating blight on crops across North America?" asked the journalist. A small window replaced the network's insignia and inside it, a male reporter wearing a light gray suit nodded to acknowledge her question as she continued. "Do we have a way to contain this fungus, and how will this affect food supplies in the immediate future?"

The small window grew to overtake the screen, and the man in the gray suit held a large microphone to his mouth. His hair blew slightly and a pale blue sky streaked with diaphanous clouds framed his head and shoulders. "We've just learned what's causing this mass infection of both wheat and corn crops across the continent. Susan, from Texas all the way through Alberta, is a scourge of what scientists and farmers alike have nicknamed 'the tombstone.' The scientific name of the fungus is *fusarium head blight*, or FHB, and it has spread like wildfire throughout the grain belt, contaminating seeds with a toxin that once ingested by livestock, has resulted in severely weakened immune systems, and in turn, has contaminated milk, beef, and chicken."

The screen split, placing Rook and Gary side-by-side like a bridal couple. Rook frowned into the camera from her vantage point in the studio. "How much of the nation's food supply has been affected, Gary?"

Gary swallowed quickly. "Susan, right now, the USDA is tracing the distribution of meat, dairy, and produce shipped from the Central Plains during the initial stages of the infection and recalling millions of items that may contain traces of the fungal toxin. They are estimating that if this spread is not contained quickly, up to seventy-five percent of the food Americans purchase at their local grocery stores may be affected and that consumers may have, in fact, purchased contaminated food unknowingly."

"Toxin on the grain. Awesome," said Aaron. "Next thing we know, the neighbors will be seeing the devil and accusing us of witchcraft."

"They are recalling all of that food? No wheat or corn products?" Cate said. "What does that leave? Peanut butter? Olive oil? Cheese?"

"Cheese is dairy," pointed out Shelley.

"Yeah, but it's been aged, so the cheese on the shelf today is probably derived from milk from before the fungus, right?" Aaron said.

"No chicken means no eggs either," said Shelley. "No baked goods. This sounds serious, guys."

"I told you," said Jess. "I'd get to the supermarket today, if I were you. You know how crazy people can get. It's gonna be survival of the fittest now." She shrugged and walked back to her bedroom door and quickly disappeared inside. The wall phone in the kitchen, the only one in the apartment, rang ceremoniously with her abrupt departure.

Cate walked to the kitchen to answer it as Aaron took a long drag from his cigarette. "Meh," he said, exhaling through his nose like a dragon, "it's just a propaganda of fear. The Republicans are pissed that the economy is improving under Clinton. Life is good. This is just a blip on the radar. There's no need for the media to go all *Animal Farm* on us."

Shelley took a swig from the vodka bottle. "*Napoleon is always right*. You betcha."

"It's for you," said Cate, stretching the extra-long cord around the doorway and handing the handset to Aaron.

He stubbed his cigarette into the ashtray on the coffee table. "Hey," he said coolly into the mouthpiece. He walked back into the kitchen, holding the phone to his ear.

Cate sat down heavily on the couch. "If it weren't the middle of winter, I'd suggest we start scavenging Coolidge Park for edible greenery."

"I'd sooner eat you than anything that is growing wild there," said Shelley, taking another drink from the bottle.

Aaron returned, a blank look plastered across his face. "I'm laid off for the next three weeks," he said. "They are changing their hours to close at five o'clock for a while."

"What?" Cate said, incredulous. "Why?"

Aaron picked up the remote control and flipped down through the channels. "There are reports of looting and riots in Worcester. Management doesn't want to be open too long after dark." He moved to the couch and sat down next to Cate, still tapping the remote with his finger. "I gotta find the local news."

Cate put her hand on Aaron's knee. "It's all going to blow over in a week or so. The U.S. can't let the nation's food supply go belly up. This is just an overreaction, like you said."

5

One evening, though, shit got real.

By the second week of February, the dingy remnants of January's Nor'easters were slowly disappearing beneath a fresh layer of snow. The weatherman had predicted fourteen inches by the time this latest snowstorm was over, and Shelley set an alarm on her watch to remind herself to leave the dissection lab before the sun had fully set. The campus was eerily empty and the streets surrounding the college were void of traffic. A lone set of tire tracks, already refilling with snow, stretched down Pearl Street, and Shelley kept her head down to keep the wind from scraping her neck as she shuffled across the road where the crosswalk had once been.

When she unlocked the door, stomping her boots on the industrial carpet before walking inside, Shelley found Aaron sitting on the couch in the living room, sipping coffee from his oversized mug and watching television, the screen casting a surreal glow in the dimly lit room. He wore only a pair of faded boxer shorts and a t-shirt, and his hair stuck out in frightful tufts like a half-blown dandelion. "It's almost five o'clock," said Shelley, shaking off her coat and unwrapping the scarf from her neck. The heat in the room was oppressive and the clumps of snow stuck to her clothing had already melted to puddles. "Are you just getting up?"

Aaron pulled a cigarette from the pack of Marlboros on the coffee table. He wedged it between his lips and lit the end before responding. "Cate kept me up most of the night." He pulled a long drag and the tip turned orange.

Shelley pulled her wet boots from her feet and lined them up against the wall near the door with only Aaron's nonslip work shoes as companions. "Where is everyone?" Shelley asked, walking toward the kitchen. The coffee pot was empty and cold. She checked the refrigerator but its only contents were a half-full tub of butter substitute and a few stray packets of fast-food ketchup. In the freezer were two empty ice trays and three open but mostly full bottles of clear liquor, lying on their side.

"Sorry," Aaron said as she returned. "This is what was left in the pot from this morning. I threw it in the microwave." He held the mug toward her but she shook her head, holding up a juice glass with an inch of vodka inside. Aaron blew a long stream of white smoke toward the industrial carpet. "Cate and Thin went to Nashua to get cigarettes and hit the grocery stores up there to see what they have." He sipped from the mug and chased it with another long drag. "The news is crazy. Check this shit." He nodded toward the screen.

Shelley sat down next to him on the couch. The CNN logo sat prominently in the lower right corner of the image as a man in a charcoal suit and red tie nodded grimly at another man wearing what appeared to be a pharmacist's white coat. "Is that Bernard Shaw?" Shelley asked. "Must be pretty big for him to be point man on a story."

Aaron shrugged. "I only know him as the guy who asked

Dukakis that question in the debate with Bush." Aaron stubbed what was left of his cigarette into the ashtray already overflowing with discarded butts.

"Turn it up," said Shelley, and Aaron complied. The shot of the reporter and interviewee dissolved into a clip of grainy footage. From the angle, it appeared to be from a grocery store security camera. "*We need to warn you,*" announced a disembodied voice, "*what you're about to see may shock some viewers. Parents of young children, please be advised: this is graphic, uncensored footage from the attack earlier this afternoon in Des Moines.*"

Shelley and Aaron squinted and leaned forward. In the lower left quadrant of the screen, a man wearing a white baseball cap removed a box from the shelf in front of him and appeared to be reading its nutritional information. A moment later, another man, this one dressed in a hooded track suit, appeared in the opposite corner. The footage was soundless, and the silence made it seem as if it were happening underwater. The second man inched slowly toward the first, his legs barely moving: a gliding motion rather than walking. The man in the cap replaced the box he was studying and picked up another one, apparently unaware of the second man's presence, even though the latter stared directly at him. In the snowy pixelation of the film, the whites of the fixated man's eyes were invisible, two round, black marbles boring holes into the fellow shopper.

"What the—" Shelley began, but Aaron held up his arm to silence her like a driver shielding his front seat passenger in a sudden brake. The second man brought his hands to his upper chest, then pulled them downward. He shook his shoulders quickly and only then was it apparent: he was removing his sweatshirt, revealing a stark, white tank top over pale white flesh underneath. The jacket fell in a clump on the floor beside him, and slowly, the man peeled his undershirt from his body as well. It wasn't until the man pushed his pants to the floor, taking his underwear with them, that the network employed a blur, disguising the man's naked genitals. Continuing to stare at the man with the baseball cap, the naked man stepped carefully from his sweatpants and took a step forward.

The man with the cap replaced the second box on the shelf in front of him and turned obliviously toward the camera lens as if preparing to continue on his way. However, as he did so, the naked man leapt from his place a few feet away and pounced on him as nimbly and ferociously as a jungle cat. For a moment, the two men disappeared from view, their spontaneous tussle occurring outside of the store's security frame. On cue, the angle changed and the perspective broadcasted from another camera pointed down an intersecting aisle. In the back of this new frame, the naked man pinned his victim to the ground; the white ball cap lay askew next to the wearer's head. A small crowd of startled onlookers creeped forward, dumbfounded, until something happened that made them all jump backwards in unison.

"Holy shit!" Aaron jumped to his feet and covered his mouth with his hand.

Although the image was grainy, there was no mistaking what the naked man was doing. He pressed his mouth against the pinned customer's cheek, closed his jaw, and tore a chunk of flesh from the man's face. Dark liquid pooled along the victim's head, and the naked man raised his own face upward as if stealing a breath, then returned to the carnage and ripped a sizable piece from the man's neck. The victim kicked and seized, trying desperately to buck his attacker and escape. On the right side of the frame, a man in a white coat inched toward the two, brandishing a cleaver.

The voiceover resumed suddenly, startling Aaron and

Shelley, who both flinched. "*We can see you now, approaching the subject*," said the reporter.

"*Uh, yeah,*" replied another voice, "*yeah...*" There was a long, awkward pause. On the screen, the naked man sat up again. Blood and sinew, black as tar, dripped from his mouth onto his chest. What had appeared to be the news report's pharmacist—now understood to be the grocery store's butcher—inched closer still, waving his weapon at the attacker, though the blade trembled in the shaken employee's hand. The second voice cleared his throat and continued. "*I just wanted to try to stop him, you know? I didn't know if the guy was dead, or if he could be saved, or what. I didn't know—*"

"What were you thinking in that moment?" asked the reporter, sternly, like a battalion leader commanding a soldier.

"Didn't he just say—" Shelley began, but Aaron made a shushing sound and held his arm out again.

The naked man returned his face to the victim, now still as stone on the supermarket linoleum. His jaw moved furiously, gnawing and chewing on the victim's shoulder, when the butcher jumped forward awkwardly and planted the blade of the cleaver in the center of the attacker's back. The screen immediately changed back to the reporter and his guest, the latter's face now as white as his jacket.

Aaron slowly sat back down.

Shelley leaned forward and tapped a cigarette out of Aaron's pack and shoved it between her lips. She laughed nervously. "I can only assume they gave him a fresh uniform to wear for the cameras. I mean ...even if he didn't get any blood on it, I would have sweat right through that one if I were him," Shelley said, then pawed the table, feeling for the plastic lighter.

Snatching it from his side of the table, Aaron lit a flame for Shelley then collapsed backward against the seat cushion.

"What the fuck is going on? Is this because of the food shortage? People are turning into goddamn *cannibals*?" As Shelley took a long drag, he gently took the cigarette from her mouth and placed it in his, inhaling sharply.

Shelley sat back as well. "Maybe it's just an amalgamation. A perfect storm, right? Like that hurricane in Gloucester a few years back. Food shortage plus cabin fever, then add a heavy hand of someone's unchecked insanity slipping through the cracks." She took back the cigarette from Aaron.

"Cabin fever?" he echoed.

"Just a guess," said Shelley. "I mean, they've suspended all classes for weeks up here, asked people to stay home if they can. It's the middle of winter and the weather's been awful: storm after storm. I can only assume it's the same everywhere. People are freaking out with worry, and now they are stuck at home. Stuck in their own heads."

Aaron took a small sip from his mug. "So they decide to start naked cannibalism rugby teams? Yeah, that tracks." He swallowed, then slapped his knee with his hand. "This is Fucked. Up. With a capital F U. Seriously."

Shelley exhaled a stream of smoke. "*This is the way the world ends. This is the way the world ends. Not with a bang—*"

"But with a crazy fucking nudist accosting you with his teeth in the middle of a Midwestern grocery store," finished Aaron, clicking the mute button on the remote control.

As if the statement's punctuation, the front door opened. "Jesus, dude," Thinny said, hefting three overstuffed brown paper bags onto the coffee table. "Turn on the news. We just heard the craziest thing on the radio."

Cate followed behind him, dumping an additional bag onto the table, then kicking off her boots and pushing them with her feet toward Shelley's. "And you have to hear about our little supermarket adventure." She took off her jacket and disappeared quickly into the women's bedroom, then returned empty-handed. "If there's ever a zombie apocalypse, Thinny here is the man in charge of our defense strategy." She flopped backwards into the well-worn recliner. Aaron began to empty the contents of the bags onto the coffee table while Thinny shook a cigarette out of the pack and sat down hard on the couch.

"What happened?" prompted Shelley. "We just saw the thing in Iowa on the news."

"We heard about it on the radio on the drive home. I mean, I hate to follow that act," said Cate. "No one got naked or tore chunks of flesh from anyone's body, but—"

"But it most definitely *could* have gone that way," interrupted Thinny. "It was a disaster in the store. Almost all of the shelves were picked over. Nothing in the frozen aisle at all. No bread, no milk, no staples at all."

"People were running all over the place," added Cate. "Driving like getaway cars in the parking lot. Filling carriages with whatever they could scavenge in the aisles and just booking it out of there."

Aaron finished emptying the last bag. "This is all you got?" The four were silent for a moment, examining the haul. On the table were five cartons of cigarettes, two four-packs of margarine, a large can of sliced mushrooms, two cans of beef stew, a crushed box of Triscuits, five canisters of powdered Kool-Aid drink mix, two boxes of spaghetti, five cans of chicken broth, a can of lima beans, and a *Maxim* magazine.

Shelley put her hand up. "I have a question. Are we frying or boiling the *Maxim*? Because I thought this was a *food run*."

"Is that Cindy Crawford topless?" Aaron asked, squinting at the cover photo.

"That's Barbara Carrera. From *The Island of Dr. Moreau*," said Thinny.

"Oh, excuse me. I didn't recognize her with someone's mittened hands covering her tits." Cate rolled her eyes. "I can't believe we came away with more cigarettes than food."

"I'll have you know," added Thinny. "There's an article on ancient sex tricks I thought we would all enjoy."

"Well, I'll be sure to peruse through it while I gnaw on a stick of Imperial," said Shelley. She tossed the magazine at Thinny's head.

Cate sighed. "I know. Trust me: I know. But we were lucky to get out with what we did. Thin had to throw his body in front of the carriage as we wheeled it back to the car. Strangers started circling us like vultures, tried to hijack the carriage and steal our bags." She shook her head. "No cops anywhere, either. No way I'm going back out again." She crossed her arms in front of her chest. "No way," she repeated.

In the kitchen, the phone rang, and Thinny got up from the couch to answer it.

Aaron sat down in Thinny's vacated spot. "Well, folks. We're going to have to start rationing. This will be over soon, but in the meantime, we can just hit the dining halls. They have a cash option. We'll survive. Besides, it's wintertime: we'll have a lot of layers on. We can definitely pilfer some food from the dining hall buffets to bring home."

Cate leaned forward. "I'd say we should just head home for the next two weeks, but it's probably like Nashua everywhere now." Despite the oppressive heat, she shivered. "Besides, I don't want to go anywhere the way things are. People are turning certifiably mad."

"I blame mad cow," deadpanned Aaron.

"*We all go a little mad sometimes*," added Shelley.

Thinny returned to the living room. His face was pale. Stricken. "What's up?" asked Aaron.

"They closed down the dining halls," he said. "Classes are

completely canceled until further notice. The governor's enacting a shelter in place. Turn the news back on." He wandered robotically to the other side of the couch and sat down. "Guys," he said as the sound came back to life on the screen, "I think things are about to get really fucking dark."

6

They hadn't seen Jess all day. That wasn't unusual, per say, especially because she was the only one of them with her own bedroom, but since classes had not been in session for more than a month and her parents had absconded to who knows where (sailing the S.S. One Percenter to an exclusive island staffed with underage servants out of the prying eyes of the United Nations, perhaps), there seemed no rational explanation where their absentee roommate might be disappearing to each day.

When she finally materialized that evening in early March sometime after dinner, the four others, having split the last box of macaroni and cheese from their stash at the top of the pantry closet, were flopped on the couch and chairs in the main room in a mild carbohydrate coma as a telethon to raise money for public television played incessantly on the television screen. They watched as she carried past them a large blue duffel bag, its contents packed so tightly they nearly split the seams. She nodded in their direction but said nothing, darting quickly in front of the television and toward her room's entrance at the back of the kitchen.

"What's in the bag?" Thinny called half-heartedly, his eyes focused on the coffee table as he sifted another pinch of marijuana into a strip of folded rolling paper. It was unclear if he expected, or even wanted, a response.

Shelley craned her neck to get a better look at the load Jess was carrying. The edges of sharp corners were visible beneath its nylon sides. "What are those? Books?"

"Mmm," Jess replied, opening her bedroom door and walking inside. She didn't turn on the light until after the door was shut, a glowing underline suddenly appearing atop the edge of linoleum. Shelley continued to watch the closed door as a shadow paced back and forth along the strip.

"Where has she been going?" Cate whispered, sitting forward on the couch to stare at the closed door off the kitchen. "I thought she would have gone home by now. I mean, no one's at her house, but it has to be a better set-up than here."

"People with money live in fortresses," said Thinny, licking the edge of the rolling paper and twisting the joint. "Like with a moat and shit." He placed it between his lips and lit the end.

"She's not a goddamn Arthurian time traveler," said Aaron, taking the joint. "But at the very least, she's gotta have a kitchen stocked with tons of food at home. A wine cellar. I mean, fuck the fall of the Berlin Wall: some of those billionaires still have working bomb shelters, I'm sure."

"I doubt she comes from *that* much money," said Shelley, keeping her voice low. "I mean, this is a state school. And anyway," she paused as Aaron passed the joint her way, "she's been bringing bags of *something* into her room for weeks now. Every goddamn night, another bundle of something. Something square and big." She inhaled deeply, holding the smoke in her lungs for as long as she could stand it as she stretched her arm out toward Thinny. "What's your take, Cate?"

"I think you're all pretty stupid to be getting high when we have nothing to eat in the house," said Cate. "What are you going to do when you get the munchies?"

Aaron leaned closer to his girlfriend and pretended to nibble on her neck, causing Cate to giggle. "I'm sure we'll figure it out," he said as she swatted him away playfully.

"Hey," said Thinny, leaning forward earnestly. "We should ask her if we can all just head down to her house." He took another long drag of the joint and inhaled sharply. "Seems like a viable option."

Shelley lowered her voice to a whisper. "Don't you think if that were a possibility she would have offered? Or at the very least, gotten the hell out of Dodge and gone there by herself by now?" She sniffed. An unpleasant odor of something sweetly rotten wafted into the room, one she'd been smelling off and one for the past month. "That smell. Is it coming from your bedroom?" she asked Aaron.

Aaron shrugged and passed the marijuana to her.

Shelley frowned. "No, I'm serious. You don't smell that? I swear: it's coming from your bedroom." She took a drag. "Cate?" she asked.

On the television screen, the emcee blathered on about maintaining access to educational programming. A ten-second promo for the network flashed by, then the screen swelled into a periwinkle background and a fluffy-haired man in jaunty white coveralls carrying an oversized paintbrush traipsed joyfully into view.

Cate yawned and lay sideways, her head resting lazily in Aaron's lap. "I'm still hungry," she said softly.

"I love Bob Ross," said Thinny.

In the kitchen, the phone trilled.

"Not it," said Shelley, passing the joint back to Aaron. Her stomach gurgled. The macaroni and cheese had been her only meal that day.

"Fuck it. Let the machine get it," said Aaron, gently stroking Cate's hair.

After two more rings, the metallic click of the answering machine chimed, followed by Cate's voice, hollow and semi-smothered in the constraints of the small speaker. "*You've reached us but we're not here. Leave a detailed message after the beep and one of us will get back to you.*" A half-hearted tone sounded, followed by a pause. Then, absurdly loud, an unfamiliar voice echoed along the kitchen walls.

"*Jessica, this is your mother. I'm just calling to let you know, we've decided to head to Delia's new place in London. We've taken Chuckie with us so don't worry about the kennel. Love you, Jessi—*"

The bedroom door off the kitchen swung open and Jess leaped from her doorway over to the phone on the wall, nearly ripping it from its cradle. "Mom?" she called into the receiver. "Mom?!" After a long pause, she smashed the receiver back into its nest, then removed it again, pressing the buttons frantically. She held the handset to her head and listened a moment before starting to speak. "Mom? It's Jess. You can't have gone already: you just left me a message. I missed your call by a half second. Please pick up." She waited a moment. "Mom? Pick up." Another second. "Pick up, pick up, pick up. Mom!!" Frustrated, she slammed the handset down. "What the FUCK?!" Jessica screamed, stomping her foot twice before running back into her bedroom and whipping the door closed.

In the living room, Thinny turned his head and looked glassy-eyed at Shelley. "Who's Chuckie?"

"The dog," Shelley whispered. "Remember? We watched the Westminster dog show that one Sunday, and she was like, *hey, that's Chuckie* during the toy breed category?"

"Her dog was in the Westminster dog show? That's pretty impressive," said Aaron.

Thinny blew a stream of smoke into the air. "She's got a fucking moat. I'm telling you." He leaned down to fumble with the last vestige of pot in the nearly obliterated roach. "And her mom sounds like a *super* nice lady..."

Shelley's stomach growled so ferociously, she felt her abdomen vibrate. "I'm going to bed," she said, standing up and walking toward the door to her room. She didn't feel like brushing her teeth or washing her face. She just wanted to curl up and sleep for a thousand years. To be awoken when the food fungus disaster was over to find the world shiny and new, their kitchen cabinets replenished, and the growing fatigue in her bones lifted.

"*Mother, Mother, I'm hungry, I'm bleeding, I'm starving to death, everything's great—*" Thinny began, mangling the lyrics to a song they had listened to earlier in the night.

"I feel like that would be a whole different song if Tracy Bonham wrote it today," said Aaron. "I mean, literally, today. In this apartment. With our last box of food obliterated."

Shelley didn't bother to close the door. She lay on her bed, squeezed her eyes closed, and pulled the comforter around her shoulders, the metronomic inflection of Bob Ross' narration stage-whispering to her from the other side of the wall. When she opened her eyes again, she was in the psychiatric hospital, lying in a bed a few feet from her stepmother's.

Diane leaned sideways and winked at Shelley. As she did so, she reached back to pull back the edge of her pillow to reveal a hidden storage of secret accruements. "Shhh." Diane put her finger to her lips, then winked slyly at Shelley, nodding downward toward her hidden treasure.

Shelley's eye drifted down to the mattress. Diane wasn't hiding sea glass below her pillow; instead, in a neat, oval-shaped pile lay a collection of human teeth, most of them yellowed or broken, many cracked and chipped to create sharp edges.

Shelley jerked her head away in revulsion and caught sight of her own frail body lying naked on the white sheet. Her breasts appeared deflated and sagged flat as pancakes pressed pathetically to her breastbone. Just below them, fish-bellied stripes delineated sharp ribs rippling down her upper torso, a silent surface of water gently whispered to by the wind and culminating in a final bank above her abdomen. Her belly button sunk to the bottom of a shallow, empty pool. Shelley ran her hand along a prominent hip bone as it curved down into her pelvis.

Diane leaned further still, her upper body precariously balanced in a vehement fight to keep from toppling forward onto the cold floor. She cleared her throat, speaking finally with a voice as ragged and coarse as the edges of her grotesque acquisitions.

"Sometimes," she whispered, the words sloshing around her throat, "sometimes, it has nothing to do with hunger at all." Then, she smiled conspiratorially at her stepdaughter, revealing a mouth of triangle shark teeth, a denticulation comprised not of human enamel but of granite, mica, and sandstone: crisp shards of calcified earth speckled with gray marbling and black pinpricks.

In a split-second, Diane pounced onto the floor between the two beds, then poked her head up just inches from Shelley's and smiled, the tips of her jagged incisors dripping with fresh saliva. "I'm starving," she said, then emitted a low, nearly imperceptible growl before her head darted quickly forward and Diane clamped her mouth tightly on her stepdaughter's upper arm.

When Shelley woke up, the light from the living room still

beamed blue and yellow in the open doorway, but there was no sound. Shelley pushed the comforter aside and padded into the next room to find the room empty, all of her roommates having absconded elsewhere. A silent Bob Ross merrily added another tree to the darkened forest of his watercolor landscape.

7

Cate sat at the kitchen table, nursing a mug of hot Kool-Aid, when Shelley wandered into the room and filled a glass of water at the faucet. "You know," Cate said, blowing on her cup before taking a small sip, "this isn't half bad, as far as steaming cups of caloric desperation is concerned."

Shelley sat down across from her. "We used to eat Jell-O packets when I was a kid, me and the neighborhood girls I played house with."

Cate rested the mug on the table and brushed her hands together. "Jell-O packets?"

Shelley took a sip of water. "Yeah, you know, the stuff you add boiling water to? The full sugar kind. We'd play kitchen and pour the powder into the little teapot, dump it into those small teacups, even pour it into play cereal bowls and scoop it up like it was real food." She tapped her finger against her glass. "We used cherry most often. Sometimes lime or orange, but I distinctly remember the cherry because it was a bitch to clean up. It was fine, super fine, like beach sand, and it stained everything: the plastic toy cups and bowls, the little wooden table we'd sit at. We'd have red lips, red fingers, red splotches all over our shirts." She smiled. "Boy, was my dad pissed. Plus, it was sticky, you know? Once just a tiny bit of it got the least bit wet, it became bright red syrup."

Cate grimaced. "Do you know what that stuff is made of? Horse hooves." She lifted the mug to her lips and took an apprehensive sip, the steam rising up to fog her glasses.

"Why did you boil it?" Shelley asked, grabbing the neck of her own t-shirt and pulling it rhythmically away from her body. "It feels about a hundred and five degrees in here as it is." She stopped pulling at her top and thought for a moment. "I could go for a big bowl of cherry Jell-O. With a ton of whipped cream."

Cate held her hand up. "First of all, we agreed not to do that. It'll be hard enough getting by on what Thinny manages to scramble up." The government had opened food distribution pantries two weeks earlier across the city, but as the five were not permanent residents and maintained driver's licenses attached only to their respective hometowns, and since they could not show photo identification proving their apartment residency, they were turned away. Luckily, Thinny said he would be able to siphon a few rations from his family's house, an hour's drive away in Boston, but most likely, it would only be enough to keep them from total starvation. "Second, that's gross. *Horse hooves.* Ew, ew, ew."

"He'll be back tonight, right?" Shelley rolled her eyes. "I mean, my head is killing me, and I didn't even drink last night," she said.

"I've had a headache for a month straight," said Cate. "I'm exhausted, but no matter how much I sleep, I'm still tired." She propped her elbows on the table and buried her face in her hands. "I think it's starting to affect my thinking," she continued, her voice slightly muffled behind her palms.

"Sometimes—I don't know—I get these thoughts, these weird thoughts that—"

"I don't know how you sleep in that room in the first place," said Shelley dismissively. "It smells like a dumpster." As she said this, Aaron walked into the kitchen. "I mean, seriously, what the hell is making that smell?" Shelley asked him, a bit more aggressively than she initially intended.

Aaron opened a cabinet and stared blankly inside. "I don't know. Probably one of Cate's vomit cans."

"You don't know?" Shelley stood up from the table. "Do you have a portal to Narnia in there, C. S. Lewis? How have you not discovered a trash can full of puke?" She moved closer to him and let her eyes follow the direction of his. Seeing only Thinny's half-full jar of shrooms and an expanse of empty shelf, Shelley grabbed Aaron's arm and shook it, frustrated. "What are you looking at?!"

"I'm hoping something will magically appear, all right?" Aaron replied angrily, shaking off her grasp. "I'm fucking starving. If you're so consumed by the smell of my bedroom, why don't YOU go in and clean it?!"

Cate lifted her head, stood up quickly, and wedged her body between them. "Listen: we are all a little short-tempered these days," she began. "I think we—"

A loud crash sounded from the set of windows next to the table as the middle pane broke open, a dark object sailing through the glass, shattering it into confetti over the tabletop. A hunk of cement tumbled onto the floor and landed next to Cate's foot. As Aaron bent down to retrieve it, a pair of faces appeared at the bottom of the opening: two boys aged twelve or thirteen years old with pale hair and skin. Their urgent breathing made quick puffs of smoke tumble into the frigid late March air. One boy smiled wickedly at Shelley as he pushed himself up and onto the sill and leaned his dirt-streaked countenance through the frame and into the apartment.

"What the fuck?" Cate said. "Get out of here!" She snatched her still-steaming mug from the table and sloshed the hot liquid onto the intruder's face.

The boy shrieked in response and backed away, losing his balance and toppling backward onto the ground a few feet below. The second boy, taller than the first, pushed himself onto the sill and crouched, kicking the remaining window glass from the frame before stepping halfway inside. "You got food," the boy said sinisterly. Not a question but a statement. He bared his top teeth in a makeshift smile, then growled like a feral animal. Shelley felt something heavy plummet to the bottom of her stomach. There was a streak of something dark red on his face that extended over his mouth. It looked like barbecue sauce, but Shelley wasn't certain that it was.

Aaron grabbed the mug from Cate's hand and held it menacingly over his head as if he meant to smash it into the boy's skull. "Does it look like we have any food? Get out of here. Now. NOW!" Aaron stepped quickly forward, and the boy slid sideways and jumped nimbly down to the ground, his head still plainly visible in the broken pane. A gust of cold wind rushed in through the wide opening, and Shelley instinctively clutched her arms to her chest to keep from shivering.

"Go bother someone else," yelled Aaron.

The boys glanced at each other quickly, then turned and walked back up the alleyway toward the street. "You're the only one left," the first kid called back at them before both boys disappeared from sight.

Cate slumped back into the chair. "It's official. We're living in *The Village of the Damned*."

Aaron put the empty mug down on the table, hard, then turned and walked toward the front door.

"Where are you going?" Cate asked.

"To scavenge for plywood in the garage," he said. "We gotta board this up before it gets dark."

"What does he mean, we're *the only ones left*?" Shelley asked.

The door to Jess' bedroom opened, and Jess stood in the doorway, brandishing a claw hammer. "What happened?" she asked. "I heard glass breaking."

Aaron walked back to the kitchen and toward her. "Just some kids." He picked up the chunk of broken sidewalk and placed it gingerly on the kitchen table. Then he walked closer to the fifth roommate and held his hand out. Jess quickly pulled the door closed behind her and stood in front of the knob. "Could I borrow the hammer?" Aaron asked. "To nail up the broken window."

"Oh," Jess said, appearing relieved. "Yes, here." She turned the tool around and held it toward Aaron with the handle facing out.

"What do you have in your room?" Cate said suddenly. Her voice was loud, as if she wanted to make absolutely certain everyone in the room heard her question.

Jess quickly folded her arms in front of her chest, tucking the hammer snugly under one arm. "What? What do you mean?"

"I mean," Cate stood up again and positioned herself immediately in front of Jess, so close that she could touch her. In response, Jess reached backward with her one empty hand and grasped the doorknob tightly.

Shelley put her hands on her hips. "She means, do you have *food* in there?" she asked, slowly understanding. "That's it, isn't it? You never join us for dinner. We never see you eat anything. You just leave and go...well, who the hell knows where you go...and then you skulk into the house every night with mysterious bundles of...what?" She took a step toward Jess.

Jess held up her hand with the hammer and pointed the claw first at Cate, then at Shelley. "Stay the hell away from me." Without looking backwards, she turned the doorknob slowly and pushed the door slightly ajar with her shoulder. Before anyone could respond, Jess sidled back into her room and slammed the door on her roommates, locking the barricade tight with an audible click.

"I hope there's a hammer in the garage," Aaron said dryly, walking toward his own bedroom door.

"What did that kid mean, we're the only ones left?" Cate called after him. Shelley said nothing but kept her eyes on Jess's closed door.

Aaron returned, sliding his arm into an overcoat. "Everyone went home, Cate. Home, or...who knows where. Somewhere with food, I'd guess. They just aren't here anymore. The streets around campus are like a ghost town, and can you blame people? We've been trapped, for the most part, in this apartment now for almost two months." He pointed to the ceiling. "I'm surprised they didn't turn off the cable when they left, but thank God for small favors, I guess." He paused and stared at Cate, waiting for her to respond. When she said nothing, he turned toward the front door. "Let me see what I can do about this window."

Shelley picked up the hunk of cement from the table and rolled it around in her hand. She looked at Jess's door.

Cate sat back down on the kitchen chair and slowly pushed the shards of glass on the table into a pile. As soon as Aaron shut the front door behind him, she chuckled softly to herself. "We're all going to die here, aren't we?" she asked, her voice barely rising above a whisper.

Shelley said nothing. She was still staring at the closed bedroom door.

Later that night, Aaron and Shelley sat on the couch, staring lethargically at the television screen, smoking cigarettes. The local news anchor smiled broadly into the camera lens as she summarized the most recent string of riots at a nearby mall.

"No one on TV seems skinnier," Shelley said. "Did you ever notice that?" She stubbed her cigarette into the ashtray, adding to the pile of spent butts piled within. The putrid smell of the dirty container wafted toward her. Incongruously, her stomach growled in response. "Why is that, do you suppose?"

Aaron continued to stare at the screen and only shrugged. The anchorwoman's smile disappeared and the screen dissolved into commercial. An actor sat at a table in front of a field of tall, green plants. He scooped his hand into an obnoxiously large bowl of brown sugar. "*It takes the best brown sugar to make a really tasty ham,*" the actor crooned enthusiastically, the camera panning to focus on a stack of pre-packaged deli meat next to him.

Cate returned from the bathroom but stopped abruptly in front of the television to stare at the image.

"*Our ham is slow baked in its own natural juices.*" The actor's voice slithered seductively through the voiceover. "*Just look at this slice!*"

Cate swallowed audibly and continued walking over to the recliner. Slowly, as if wincing in pain, she curled her legs up beneath her and rested the side of her face against the headrest. Aaron leaned forward and shook another cigarette out of the pack and lit it with the one he just finished.

"Funny that the tobacco crop wasn't affected by the blight," Cate said to no one in particular.

On the screen, the actor raised a roll of sliced ham to his mouth. "*Low in fat,*" he said gleefully and took a bite. "*Just taste the difference!*"

Aaron blew a long stream of smoke in his direction. "Thank Christ," he said.

The actor chewed through his smile. "*Mmmmmm,*" he purred. "*So good.*"

The three were silent for a beat, all of them earnestly watching, hypnotized.

"*That sweet brown sugar,*" continued the actor. "*It's so, so good.*"

Cate cleared her throat. "It's cold in the kitchen," she said. "Why is it so cold in there? I thought you covered the window." Mercifully, the screen image changed to Cindy Crawford frolicking around a beach, kissing random strangers.

"I remember reading somewhere that Johnny Depp said that loved smoking so much, he wished he had a second mouth so that he could shove another cigarette into it," Shelley said. She rubbed her bottom lip with her index finger. "Right now, I'd quit cold turkey for a cheeseburger. I'd give my *right hand* for a cheeseburger with extra ketchup."

Aaron uttered a forced chuckle. "If you gave your right hand, I'd take it," he said. "And I'd throw it on the cast iron pan and sauté it." He took a long drag and turned to look at Cate. "I couldn't find any plywood, so I just cut up some boxes with my razor from work and taped it up with the cardboard."

"I think we're out of margarine sticks," said Shelley. "My hand would burn."

"Meh," said Aaron. "I'm sure we could scare up a can of that nonstick spray from somewhere."

Cindy Crawford kissed a young boy on the cheek then triumphantly pointed to his skin to show she hadn't left a lipstick mark.

"Ketchup or no?"

"Most definitely. Maybe a little Frank's Red Hot—"

"Shut up, both of you. Shut up!" Cate stood up and screamed at the two of them. "I'm tired of feeling like this! I'm tired of being so goddamn exhausted! My head, my head is killing me, and...Please? Can you just cut it out? At least until Thinny comes with the food." Her voice trailed off at the end, like a wind-up toy running slowly out of juice.

Aaron laughed. He took a longer drag on his cigarette and laughed harder, choking and coughing as he did so.

"What is so funny?!" Cate demanded. "What the fuck is—"

Aaron's laughter stopped abruptly. "Thinny isn't *coming* back, don't you get it?" he said, his voice flat. He focused his eyes back on the television. The news anchor reappeared, the toothy smile plastered across her countenance once more.

Shelley looked down at the coffee table. She knew Aaron was right. She had known it when she saw Thinny throw all of his dirty laundry into a sack before slinging the bag over his shoulder and heading toward the front door. He had looked at her for a long time before saying goodbye.

"What..." Cate looked at Shelley, then at Aaron. "But we have *nothing* here. How..." Her voice trailed off again, the anchorwoman's droning recital the only sound in the room once more. The three watched the rest of the news program in uncomfortable silence.

When the screen dissolved to commercial again, Cate leaned forward in the chair and spoke in a clear, loud tone. "I can't die like this, starving to emaciation," she said.

Aaron leaned forward as well. He slid another cigarette out of the pack but did not put it in his mouth, only tapped the tip of it against the table top. "What was it that Cobain wrote in his suicide note? *It's better to burn out than fade away*?" he said.

"He stole it from Neil Young," said Cate.

"I thought he stole it from Joe Elliott," Shelley said.

"You thought Kurt Cobain was quoting Def Leppard?" Cate said incredulously. She didn't wait for a response but instead added, "How long can someone go without food? You're the biology major."

Shelley sniffed. "Three days maximum without water, but we have plenty of that," she said. "A couple of months without any food at all."

"It's already been three weeks," Cate said. "I have to find something to eat."

Aaron stood up. "Let's just go to bed, Cate. I'm tired. You're tired. Let's just get some sleep and talk about this in the morning." He clicked the remote control to turn off the television, walked over to his girlfriend, and pulled gently on her sweater. "We can get up early and do some errands, look around for open grocery stores before the crazies come out for the day."

Shelley stood up as well. "I'm beat. I'm headed for bed, too."

Cate pulled her arm away from Aaron's grasp. "I'll be there in a little while," she said, staring at the dark screen. The three friends' images reflected in the convex surface like a funhouse mirror. "Burn out or fade away," she repeated softly.

Aaron sighed and walked slowly into his bedroom. Shelley smiled at Cate, but her roommate wasn't looking at her. She was staring at the doorway across the room on the other side of the kitchen. At the bottom of Jess's door, a single margin of light glowed.

8

Shelley woke from another nightmare with a start, her leg already halfway off of the bed in preparation for flight. In this dream, someone had been knocking at her bedroom window, and Shelley pulled up the shade to see Diane standing there, her palm pressed against the glass, the heat of her skin forming a halo of condensation around each finger.

"Diane?" Shelley asked, dumbfounded. Their apartment was on the first floor, but somehow, her stepmother's head and chest were even with Shelley's, as if she were hovering three feet above the ground, like Ralphie in the television movie of *Salem's Lot*. She must have been four or five years old, sleepily wandering into the den to inquire for a glass of water from her father, when she caught sight of the frightful scene framed within their carved wooden TV console, and the memory had been lying in wait in the back of her memory bank ever since.

As she lay in bed, trying to recall more of the dream, Shelley did not know what Diane had done in response. Had she knocked again? Shelley thought that she had. Or perhaps she had reached through the glass, invited herself inside, the shark teeth from previous nocturnal encounters mashing together, glistening with hungry spit.

Shelley shook her head, trying to wipe the image's remnants from her mind like an Etch-a-Sketch. She swung her other leg out from under the covers and got out of bed. The clock on her dresser read seven-thirty A.M.. From the margins of her drawn shades peeked the eerie bluish light of a late winter sunrise, and as she walked softly into the living room and kitchen, Shelley relied on the muted glow of the morning sky through the windows to light her way.

There was an unfamiliar odor in the living room, something metallic, slightly sweet and wet smelling, but Shelley brushed it off as a mixture of stale cigarette smoke, months of marathon couch sitting, and her own stomach acid pleading for closure. It was likely the ketosis she was smelling, her own insides gnawing on themselves for sustenance.

As she pulled a glass from the cabinet, the toilet flushed; a moment later, Jess emerged from the bathroom, startled by Shelley's presence. As Shelley filled her glass with water, her roommate sidled by, sidestepping her cautiously like a frightened animal. She paused at her bedroom door, pressing her back to it.

Shelley took a long drink, messily dripping water down the side of her chin, then wiped her mouth on the sleeve of her shirt. "Morning," she said dully. She lifted the glass back to her mouth.

"Morning," replied Jess. "Looks like it's just us girls now. Aaron left."

Shelley swallowed quickly. "What? No, he didn't."

"Yeah," Jess said, shifting uncomfortably. "I just saw Cate a few minutes ago. I think she's headed to the laundromat. She was coming out of the bathroom with all but one of the towels. 'Said Aaron decided to go home last night."

"He wouldn't do that," Shelley said. "He wouldn't just leave and not say goodbye, and certainly not in the middle of the night like he's wanted by the feds or something."

Jess shrugged and looked away. "I don't know what to tell you," she said quickly. Her arms remained behind her back, and she rolled her shoulders back nervously but did not make a move to retreat back into her room.

Shelley put the glass of water down on the counter. "What do you have in there?" she asked. "Seriously: enough is enough, Jess. At this point, I could give two fucks about your fortress of secrecy." Shelley put one hand on a hip and stared at her roommate.

There was a short, awkward silence. Then, Jess cleared her throat. "It's my room. It's none of your business." She didn't look up but instead focused her eyes on the cardboard covering the window and frowned.

Shelley followed her line of vision. The chunk of cement from the day before was still on the table. She took a deep breath. "If that's how you want it..." she said, trying to keep her voice even. Like a cat, however, she leaped forward, then held her hands, palms up, in front of her like a riot shield. With the last of her reserve energy, Shelley pushed Jess as hard as she could, knocking her into the door and forcing it open. Without stopping to flip on the light inside, she continued to bulldoze Jess forward with her body until the two of them stumbled over something angular but lightweight on the floor below. Shelley felt her roommate fall and heard the soft crash of her body hitting whatever was piled behind her. Before the woman could recover, Shelley reached her hand backwards to feel along the inside wall for the switch.

Shelley blinked several times against the glare of the hundred-watt bulb. For a moment, she simply scanned the contents of the room in disbelief.

Rock of Ages

Piled in haphazard towers against every wall were boxes of every color. Cereal boxes. There were hundreds, perhaps even a thousand boxes of cereal, every type of cereal: whole grain and artificially sweetened, flakes and pillowy squares, cinnamon-sugared or chocolate coated, tossed with pastel marshmallows or mingled with dried fruit. More than half of the boxes were unopened, stacked horizontally so that their sealed tops were clearly visible in the multicolored array. Behind and beneath Jess, still sprawled backward on the floor, were the now disheveled stacks of flattened, empty cereal boxes: at least a hundred cardboard carcasses. On Jess's nightstand and strewn about her mattress were three or four newly opened boxes, their plastic innards sticking halfway out of them like disemboweled murder victims.

The whole room smelled stiflingly sweet, like a bakery. Shelley inhaled deeply and swallowed the tidal wave of saliva flooding her mouth. "Where—where did you get all of these?" She turned to the tower closest to the door. It nearly touched the ceiling.

"My parents own a food manufacturing company," said Jess quietly. She told Shelley the name. It was one Shelley had seen staring back at her from the sides of cereal boxes she had eaten from as a child. On *every* box of cereal she'd eaten as a child. Jess' parents didn't just have some money. They had more money than they could ever spend in a lifetime.

It's gonna be survival of the fittest now.

Shelley's stomach gurgled. She felt the acid bubble up into her esophagus, and she spun around to look at Jess. "You...you had all of this food, and you kept it to yourself?!" She raised her foot and briefly considered kicking Jess squarely in the mouth but instead struck her toe at a nearby pile of flattened boxes. An errant container with a cartoon sea captain sporting a white mustache sailed under Jess's bed. "You—you are a fucking *monster*."

Shelley spotted the hammer Jess had been holding the previous day. She snatched it from the desk where it sat and walked immediately over to the bedroom door. Over and over, she slammed the hammer's head into the lock Jess had installed. She continued striking the lock as hard as she could until the latch came free and dislodged from the frame. Her arm screaming with pain, Shelley tossed the hammer under Jess's bed, then ran through the kitchen and across the living room. "Aaron!" Shelley called. "Aaron! You have to fucking see this—"

Shelley opened Aaron's closed door, not bothering to knock. She was three steps into the room before a very different sort of scent filled her nostrils. The stench she had been smelling for months was much stronger inside of the room, and it had changed somehow. It no longer smelled like something rotting but instead, there was a sweetness in the aroma, a metallic undertone, like warm pennies.

All of the window shades were still drawn in the room, so Shelley walked slowly forward and felt along the first nightstand to turn on a lamp. Directly in front of her was the side of Aaron's bed, a heavy comforter thrown awkwardly atop the mattress. In front of the nightstand stood a metal trash can, the pastel cartoon of My Little Pony on its side. Shelley glanced inside. At the bottom of the bin was a thin layer of hardened vomit, long crusted over with a fuzzy blanket of white and black mold.

"Shelley." Cate's voice was scratchy and weak. Shelley did not see her roommate anywhere, but the sound had come from the other side of the bed, from somewhere on the floor. "Shelley," the voice repeated. "Don't come in here. Please. Go back to the kitchen. I can explain..."

Shelley's eyes adjusted to the dim light and she quickly scanned the room. Just beyond the edge of the comforter, the top of Cate's head surfaced, her ginger red hair glowing almost magenta in the incandescence. Shelley walked to the foot of the bed. "Cate? What's going on? I saw what Jess has in her room. I saw—"

She stopped walking. On the floor in front of the bed was more vomit: this time, still liquid but congealing. It was tinged with streaks of pink and red. Beyond the rancid-smelling puddle, though, was something else: Aaron's feet and the bottom of his shins lay completely still on the rug on the other side of the bed.

Shelley walked slowly and carefully around the vomit, covering her mouth and nose with her hand. The odor grew progressively thicker with each step she took, but she continued forward. When she saw what had previously been hidden, however, Shelley stepped backwards on instinct, nearly slipping in the wet sick before righting her body and forcing herself to look at the gruesome scene again.

Cate was bent over on her knees. In her hands was a bath towel, one that had once been a light shade of blue but now appeared dark brown in most places. Cate pressed the towel over and over into the rug in front of her, absorbing more of the enormous, dark stain: a stain, Shelley quickly realized, made by blood. Aaron's blood.

On the rug, Aaron lay on his back, his eyes open, staring drowsily at the ceiling, unblinking. He wore only his tattered boxer shorts and white gym socks. Above the waist of his underwear, his chest was wet and darkly sticky. Pieces of his chest, Shelley realized, were missing. Long strips of flesh had been cut away: deep cuts revealing the moist sinew beneath. The white edge of a rib glistened like the inside of a seashell from the center of the carnage. Most of the skin and muscle was missing from his left arm as well, and below the elbow, the flesh had been torn away almost completely. Beside his left pinky finger lay a steel box cutter—Aaron's, from work, Shelley guessed—painted heavily with blood, most of it dried to thick globs of reddish-black.

Shelley stared at her friend's mutilated corpse in disbelief. It wasn't until a full minute had passed that she recognized a shape clearly outlined along the edge of Aaron's shoulder. It was a human bite impression: a full set of upper and lower choppers, neatly branded into what little was left of his skin in the upper torso.

Finally catching up to what her eyes had absorbed, Shelley's stomach contracted violently in rebellion. She turned her back on her dead friend and made her own contribution to the puddle of puke on the floor—though, to be fair, it was mostly brown-tinted water. Cate began to sob. She sat back on her heels and buried her face in her hands.

Shelley spat and wiped her mouth with the back of her hand. She couldn't look at Cate. She couldn't look at Aaron, either, so instead, she focused her eyes on the bloody razor tool. A small flap of skin was wedged in the crevice between the blade and the handle. When she could finally speak, the stomach acid in her throat made the words feel like gravel. "Jesus Christ. Jesus Christ, Cate. What did you do? What did you do?!"

Cate wiped her face with her hands and turned to look at Shelley. There were wet brown streaks across her cheeks and down her neck. Her pupils were absurdly large, the blackness of them nearly swallowing her blue irises whole. "I don't know... I don't—I..." She swallowed. "Last night, Aaron fell asleep right away, and I just couldn't. My stomach felt like it was caving in on itself. I was lying in bed, and I kept thinking. Like, maybe we missed something. Maybe we shoved some food—a box or a can—into the back of one of the cabinets and missed it. So, I got up, started rummaging around the kitchen, trying to find something—anything—to eat. And they were right there, you know?"

"What?" Shelley asked. "What was there?"

"Thinny's mushrooms," Cate explained. "He didn't take them home with him. I think he forgot them. He must have. It wasn't like the rest of us were dipping into his stash or anything." She wiped her face again, leaving another line of dried blood; this time, along her forehead. "I thought, I'll just eat a few. I'll eat a few and then there will be something in my stomach at least, and then I can stop thinking about it. I took one from the jar and put it in my mouth and started chewing. It tasted awful—truly awful—but bigger than the taste was the sensation, the feeling of having food on my tongue again: it just felt…right. Truth be told, it felt *amazing* just to be eating again. So I ate another, and another, and before I knew it, I had eaten all of them, emptied the jar."

Shelley stared at Cate. "You ate *all* of the shrooms in that jar? All of them?"

"Yes," said Cate quickly. "And by that time, I was completely awake. There was no way I was going to sleep, so I figured I'd watch some TV or something. I drank a glass of water, brushed my teeth, went into the living room and tried to tidy it up a bit. But then there was this sound, you know? The apartment was so quiet, but I swore I heard this sound coming from Aaron's room. A whistling, but not really whistling…more like, a *sizzling*."

Cate's speech increased in speed and she became more and more animated as she recounted this, her exaggerated hand gestures and black eyes making her look like a demented children's show puppet. Shelley carefully took a step backwards and looked cautiously toward the door.

"...I began creeping quietly all over the room, looking for the source of that sizzling, you know? It sounded like...it sounded like butter on a hot griddle, and then—I swear to you, Shell—I thought I actually *smelled* butter cooking for a second. But another part of me thought, what was a rational explanation for that sound, that smell? Maybe there was an electrical fire or an outlet frying or something. I turned on the lamp and looked around, and there was Aaron, lying on the bed, holding out his arm toward me." Cate began to laugh: a high-pitched, mad giggle. "Except it wasn't his arm, you see? It was the cast iron frying pan. He had gotten it from the kitchen and heated it up, and he had found us food, Shelley: real food!"

Shelley's eyes darted around the room. There was no pan anywhere in sight. "Hold on, wait a second," she said, holding up a finger before turning to leave the room. She ran quickly to the kitchen. Sure enough, the cast iron frying pan was still on its hook. Shelley removed it from its hanger and ran her palm along its side. A thin layer of dust piled up beside her thumb.

"This pan?" Shelley asked, returning to the room and holding it out toward Cate accusingly. "This is the pan Aaron was holding, that he was frying butter in?"

Cate frowned. "Well, no. Because as soon as he held it out toward me, he stopped holding the pan. Instead, his hand *was* the pan. Don't you get it? His whole forearm became the pan, handle and all, this robotic extension extending out from his elbow. And inside, inside of the pan there was food: Aaron had cooked something just for us, and I wanted to wait, you know? I wanted to be polite and wait, but I was just so *hungry*, so I grabbed the handle and tried to take the pan from him, but he kept wrestling it away from me, saying I couldn't eat it, what did I think I was doing? The whole time, the smell kept getting stronger, that smell of butter, and drool was coming out of the sides of my mouth, and all Aaron kept saying was *Stop! Stop! Stop!* He was practically yelling it, and I just wanted him to give me the pan, just to give me a little taste and for Christ sakes, to *stop fucking yelling*, so I grabbed the pillow and I shoved it over his face and sat down on it as hard as I could..." Cate paused and thought for a moment, staring blankly at the side of the mattress. "It was the box cutter on the nightstand. I remember thinking, if I could just cut the pan off of Aaron's arm, I could take it into the kitchen, and Aaron could just stay here and no one would have to know. I could have the food all to myself, you know? No one would have to know..."

Shelley stared at her. A heavy silence hovered between them for a long minute.

Cate looked down at her hands. "It felt so good to eat again. And once I started, I couldn't stop," she said, her voice dropping to nearly a whisper. "I just kept eating and eating until my stomach was so full, I threw up."

Shelley glanced at the puddle of vomit.

Cate looked up at her. "And then it all went away. And Aaron..." She looked at her boyfriend's face and began to cry again. "I thought... I thought...." she began, but her voice dissolved into sobs.

Shelley looked at Aaron, too. The whites of his eyes were tinged red with broken blood vessels. "Jess has been hoarding food," Shelley said softly. "That's why she wouldn't let us in her room."

Cate's continued to cry for another minute, then stopped abruptly. "What? What did you say?"

Shelley said nothing, only looked at her.

Cate looked at Aaron again. Her eyes drifted down to his mutilated torso and over to the skeletal remains of his forearm. Very slowly, she rose to her feet and without a word, took the frying pan from Shelley's hand. She stepped gingerly around Shelley and the mess on the floor and exited the room.

Shelley looked down at Aaron for a long moment before she followed her.

Jess's bedroom door was still open, its occupant having moved from the floor to the edge of her bed. "Cate, I can explain—" she began, but Cate did not want to hear the rest of her statement.

Without saying a word, she lifted the cast iron pan above her head and brought it down on Jess's head. Jess fell backwards onto the mattress and Cate hopped quickly up to kneel beside her. Jess raised her hands in an attempt to shoo her roommate away, and Cate raised the weapon as if to strike her again. Instead, however, she turned and dropped the pan off the side of the bed and onto the floor. "What did you make me do?" Cate whispered. "What did you make me do?" She repeated this question over and over before it dissolved into sobs. Cate lay sideways on the other side of Jess's bed and curled herself into a fetal position, softly crying.

Jess didn't see Shelley enter the room. She most definitely didn't see the hunk of sidewalk Shelley held in her hand, and when Shelley struck Jess squarely in the center of her face, she did it with such savagery, such enthusiasm, Jess had no opportunity to fight her off. Shelley struck her again. And again. And again. With each blow, there was a hard crunching sound, like the shell of a walnut cracking. Shelley continued to hit Jess until her head was no longer a hard skull surrounded by flesh but a fragmented pile of puzzle pieces buried within a sticky, wet pulp.

Cate stopped crying and simply hugged her knees to her chest. Shelley dropped the rock and walked slowly, dazed, into the kitchen.

On the wall next to the refrigerator, the phone began to

ring. Instead of answering it, Shelley sat down in one of the chairs at the table. A stiff breeze hit the window, making the cardboard shiver.

Finally, the answering machine clicked to life, Cate's surrealistically cheerful voice echoing across every wall of the apartment. *"You've reached us but we're not here. Leave a detailed message after the beep and one of us will get back to you."* The metallic tone rang out, followed by a pause.

Shelley's father could be heard as clearly as if he were standing right in front of her. *"Shelley?"* He cleared his throat. *"Shelley, this is Dad. I'm calling because..."* His voice hitched a bit, stuttered, then resumed. *"Shelley, it's Diane. Diane is gone. She...she's dead, Shelley. Somehow, she managed to get a hold of a bag of—"*

Shelley hit the STOP button on the machine. In the abrupt silence, Shelley could hear Cate in the next room. She was sobbing again.

It wasn't that Diane hadn't known that rocks weren't food. It wasn't that Cate hadn't known that human beings weren't food. And if there was one thing that Shelley did know, it was that once you'd been determined to be incapable of rational thought, it was all over. There was no coming home. Not really.

Not ever.

Shelley walked calmly into the living room. Aaron's plastic lighter was on the coffee table, where it had always lived. She slid one cigarette out from the pack beside it and placed it between her lips. Her hand was bloody and left a bright red streak on the filter. Whether the mess was from Jess's body or her own, she didn't know, but she wiped her palm on the front of her shirt and continued on to Aaron's room. She calmly lit the cigarette, took a long drag, then held the lighter's flame steady along the corner of Aaron's bed comforter. When the fire began to lick the top of the mattress, she exited, walked through the kitchen and back into Jess's room.

Kurt Cobain was right. And Neil Young. And Joe Elliott, for that matter.

Cate buried her face in her hands while Shelley held the lighter against the tallest tower of cereal boxes, the one immediately next to the room's only exit, and lit the flame. She sat down on a nearby pile of empty boxes and took another long drag.

The cereal began to roast; the sugary flakes catching fire, piece by piece. *Pop, pop, pop, pop, pop.*

And Shelley's stomach growled.

THE END

ABOUT THE AUTHOR

Rebecca Rowland is the dark fiction author of two fiction collections, one novel, a handful of novellas, and too many short stories. She is the best-selling editor of seven horror anthologies, including 2023's American Cannibal. Her speculative fiction, critical essays, and book reviews regularly appear in a variety of online and print venues. The former acquisitions and anthology editor at AM Ink Publishing, Rebecca co-owns and manages the small, independent publishing house Maenad Press.

www.RowlandBooks.com

ALSO BY REBECCA ROWLAND

As Author:

White Trash & Recycled Nightmares

Optic Nerve

Shagging the Boss

The View Master

Terror for Teetotalers

The Horrors Hiding in Plain Sight

Pieces

As Editor:

American Cannibal

Dancing in the Shadows: A Tribute to Anne Rice

Generation X-ed

The Half That You See

Unburied: A Collection of Queer Dark Fiction

Shadowy Natures

Ghosts, Goblins, Murder, & Madness: Twenty Tales of Halloween

Contact one of the Texas providers listed below to learn more about nutrition programs in your area. Most service a wide range of counties outside of their immediate location.

Brazos Valley Food Bank
   979-779-3663
   1501 Independence Ave.
   Bryan, Texas 77803

Central Texas Food Bank
   512-282-2111
   6500 Metropolis Dr.
   Austin, Texas 78744

Concho Valley Regional Food Bank
   325-655-3231
   1313 South Hill St.
   San Angelo, Texas 76903

East Texas Food Bank
   903-597-3663
   3201 Robertson Rd.
   Tyler, Texas 75701

El Pasoans Fighting Hunger
   915-298-0353
   9541 Plaza Circle
   El Paso, Texas 79927

Food Bank of Corpus Christi
   361-887-6291
   826 Krill St.
   Corpus Christi, Texas 78408

Texas Food Bank Information

Food Bank of the Golden Crescent
361-578-0591
801 South Laurent St.
Victoria, Texas 77901

Food Bank of the Rio Grande Valley
956-682-8101
724 N. Cage Blvd.
Pharr, Texas 78577

Food Bank of West Central Texas
325-695-6311
5505 North 1st St.
Abilene, Texas 79603

High Plains Food Bank
806-374-8562
817 S. Ross St.
Amarillo, Texas 79120

Houston Food Bank
713-223-3700
535 Portwall St.
Houston, Texas 77029

North Texas Food Bank
214-269-0906
4500 South Cockrell Hill Rd.
Dallas, Texas 75236

San Antonio Food Bank
210-337-3663
5200 Historic Old Hwy 90

San Antonio, Texas 78227

South Plains Food Bank
806-763-3003
5605 MLK Blvd.
Lubbock, Texas 79404

South Texas Food Bank
956-726-3120
2121 Jefferson St.
Laredo, Texas 78040

Southeast Texas Food Bank
409-839-8777
3845 South ML King Jr. Parkway
Beaumont, Texas 77705

Tarrant Area Food Bank
817-857-7100
2600 Cullen St.
Fort Worth, Texas 76107

West Texas Food Bank
432-580-6333
411 South Pagewood Ave.
Odessa, Texas 79761

Wichita Falls Area Food Bank
940-766-2322
1230 Midwestern Parkway
Wichita Falls, Texas 76302

Made in United States
Orlando, FL
25 September 2023